Nicole

Desperately she pulled at Alex's tie, shoved his coat down over his arms, then dived for his belt buckle. She heard her dress rip and realized Alex was trying to gain access to her breasts. Obviously he needed this as much as she did.

Wriggling her hips to get the room she needed, she finally freed his erection. Impressive. *Very* impressive. "A condom," she said breathlessly. "Give me a condom."

Alex froze. Just froze. His mouth still rested against her breast, his erection still pulsed against her too-hot flesh. But he wasn't moving anymore. And she didn't want to know the reason.

Nicole turned away from him, feeling the incredible, confusing urge to cry as sexual frustration pressed from the inside out. She wanted to scream in disappointment. Until she felt something cold encircle her left wrist.

Handcuffs.

Nicole turned and watched as Alex fastened the other side of the handcuffs to his right wrist. Not to the bedpost on the big four-poster bed dominating the small room. *Damn.*

She collapsed on the mattress and sighed. "You don't have a condom, but you have handcuffs," she said absently. "You really need to reevaluate your priorities, man."

Dear Reader,

The edge. That's where we like to take our stories and our characters. But in our contribution to THE BAD GIRLS CLUB miniseries, we were given the opportunity to really cut loose and go farther than we ever had before. Only, not even *we* could have imagined the sexy game of cat and mouse our characters Nicole Bennett (the thief in *Private Investigations*) and Alex Cassavetis had in mind....

In *Red-Hot & Reckless,* sexy expert thief Nicole Bennett has always managed to stay one step ahead of the law, mostly because she targets other thieves, the last people who will call in the authorities. But she hasn't counted on seductive insurance investigator Alex Cassavetis stealing something from *her*. Namely her heart...

We hope you enjoy Nic and Alex's sizzling journey to the edge and beyond. We'd love to hear what you think. Write to us at P.O. Box 12271, Toledo, OH 43612, or visit us on the Web at www.toricarrington.com and www.temptationauthors.com.

Here's wishing you love, romance and hot reading.

Lori & Tony Karayianni
aka Tori Carrington

Books by Tori Carrington

HARLEQUIN TEMPTATION	HARLEQUIN BLAZE
823—YOU ONLY LOVE ONCE	15—YOU SEXY THING!
837—NEVER SAY NEVER AGAIN	37—A STRANGER'S TOUCH
876—PRIVATE INVESTIGATIONS	56—EVERY MOVE YOU MAKE
890—SKIN DEEP	65—FIRE AND ICE
	73—GOING TOO FAR

Tori Carrington
Red-Hot & Reckless

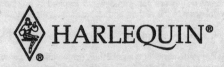

HARLEQUIN®

TORONTO • NEW YORK • LONDON
AMSTERDAM • PARIS • SYDNEY • HAMBURG
STOCKHOLM • ATHENS • TOKYO • MILAN • MADRID
PRAGUE • WARSAW • BUDAPEST • AUCKLAND

This one's for fellow Temptresses
Leslie Kelly and Julie Elizabeth Leto,
as well as our editor, Brenda Chin.

Thanks, guys, for letting us in on
how good it is to be so very, *very* bad!

ISBN 0-373-69124-6

RED-HOT & RECKLESS

Copyright © 2003 by Lori & Tony Karayianni.

Visit us at www.eHarlequin.com

Printed in U.S.A.

_____Prologue_____

NICOLE BENNETT had two weaknesses: Tiffany jewelry and men. And both were about to get her into a whole heap of trouble. The jewelry, because it wasn't actually hers. And the man, because he'd called the cops on her five minutes ago.

Nicole rushed around the shabby one-bedroom apartment that belonged to Sebastian Pollock, the bit Broadway actor she'd been dating and basically living with over the past week. She alternately wiped prints from the surfaces that weren't already covered in dust and stared out the window for the police to arrive at the hovel in the south Bronx. After hurrying her black cat named Cat into his carrier, she slung the strap over her left shoulder, and her black leather backpack over her right shoulder. Then she grabbed a 9 x 12 padded mailing envelope and tucked inside the carefully wrapped sterling silver jewelry. All along she cursed herself for ever having accused Sebastian of being a one-minute man that morning.

Using a red handkerchief, she wiped the doorknob clean, then opened it so she could step out into the hall. She gasped when she found Sebastian leaning against the wall right outside, his arms crossed over his impressive chest.

"Going somewhere?" he asked, his right brow arched high on his handsome forehead.

"Fasten your seatbelts. It's going to be a bumpy night," Nicole recited the famous Bette Davis quote, one of her favorites and definitely befitting her current circumstances.

Then again, the quote could pretty much apply to her entire life.

She made a face. What was it with her and tall, good-looking men who were about as deep as a mud puddle? Okay, so the type rarely asked questions—which was important given her line of work as a thief. But they also tended to get upset when they were offered a bit of objective criticism. In Sebastian's case, it was that the idea of sex with him was a far sight better than the real thing. Mostly because the idea lasted a whole lot longer.

Oh, well. Just another mistake in a long list of others.

Nicole thrust the heel of her hand into his solar plexus, watched as he doubled over and gasped for air, then checked his pockets for the missing piece of jewelry. There. In his right front jeans pocket. She took out the bracelet and looked at it. She grimaced at the irony of the words stamped on the smooth tag, then smiled at Sebastian as she added the piece to the contents of the mailer.

"Thanks for the memories," she said to him, quoting the sentiment on the tag.

She walked down the hall toward the back fire escape, not about to take the chance that by the time she climbed the four flights of stairs the police would be waiting for her outside. She thought about where she should go from there.

Baltimore. Definitely Baltimore.

Cat meowed and she looked down at him. "Looks like it's another visit with Auntie Danika for you, buddy," she said and picked up the pace.

1

SOMEONE WAS FOLLOWING HER.

Three days after the Sebastian episode, Nicole Bennett sat in a Baltimore, Maryland, bar called Flanagan's Pub. Not her original destination, but a spontaneous detour designed to flush out her tail.

She was pretty sure someone was watching her. Maybe had been since she'd arrived in the city the same day she'd left New York. And she was convinced that the sensation was more than residual uneasiness left over from what had happened three days ago. Still, it wasn't that she had actually spotted the person tailing her. Rather, it was more of a hunch that someone, somewhere was shadowing her moves. She could tell by the way her skin itched. How the tiny hairs on her arms stood on end. How the beer- and smoke-soaked air of the bar seemed to hum with a strange expectancy.

Her tail wasn't in the establishment. She was sure of that. It had taken her all of two seconds to catalog everything and everyone in the place. Two businessmen occupied a corner booth. When they weren't hitting on the ballsy barmaid well equipped to handle anything that came her way, they were deep in conversation, too doughy and pale to be members of any branch of law enforcement she had to be afraid of. Well, the IRS aside. But she had nothing to fear from the IRS. They wouldn't collect a percentage of what they couldn't prove she had. An elderly woman and her two middle-aged daughters bearing shopping bags occupied another booth—again, no threat, as they laughed over pints of dark Irish beer, then pulled comical faces when they tasted the bitter concoction.

Nicole looked back at the barmaid. Of course, she had initially presented a bit of concern. Her take-charge efficiency and razor-sharp wit made her the perfect candidate for either side of the legal fence. But the bar had been an unplanned stop and in Nicole's experience no branch of law enforcement was that organized.

She looked at the woman in question. She seemed distracted. More than likely a man, Nicole thought. Only a man could put a grimace like that on a woman's face. Just seeing it made her want to join in the grimacing.

"Probably moved on to the next willing female before my plane left the ground," the barmaid muttered as she wiped down the sticky surface of the bar.

Bingo.

But Nicole found very little comfort in the confirmation. Truth was, it stank to look at someone who felt pretty much the way you did.

The door opened and a well-turned-out redhead came in, her clothes and jewelry the real thing. No threat, even if Nicole suspected the woman hadn't been born to her current wealthy position. She'd been around both old money and the nouveau riche enough to tell. She automatically priced the pieces the woman wore, then dismissed them. Not because of their worth, but rather because the only jewelry Nicole targeted was Tiffany, and the only jewels she lifted were unset and most of the time uncut, easily fenced.

"Cool shirt."

Nicole glanced to see that the newcomer was talking to the barmaid, not her. Her own slick black leather pants and low-cut leather vest were world's apart from the playful T-shirt sporting a cartoon of Jessica Rabbit the barmaid had on.

"You don't look like the T-shirt type," the bartender told the newcomer.

The woman's warm laugh drew the attention of the two businessmen, as she'd almost certainly intended, probably more due to nature than design.

"Believe me, sister, I don't dress this way every day. And I certainly don't do it for myself."

The woman continued speaking, still talking about the barmaid's shirt and Jessica Rabbit. "I'd like to think I have a lot in common with her. Not bad, just drawn that way."

The barmaid nodded. "My motto." She poured a shot of the good stuff and slid it over to the latest arrival. "My name's Venus. Venus Messina."

The woman extended her hand. "Sydney. Sydney Colburn."

Nicole's attention turned from the door to the two women.

The barmaid named Venus was staring curiously at the other woman. "Sydney Colburn...no kidding? The writer?"

After Sydney tasted the whiskey, she nodded. "One and the same."

Only then did the name ring a bell with Nicole. Oh, yeah, she was familiar with the author. She'd picked up a few of Colburn's novels at airport kiosks while en route. Initially she'd done so to discourage conversation during flights. But from the first sizzling word she'd read she'd become hooked.

Venus was telling Sydney how much she liked the heroes in Sydney's novels, saying it was too bad more men couldn't live up to that standard, then added, "And my favorite part. No wimpy heroines!"

"Men who meet my standard do exist," the author said softly. "The trouble is finding them."

Nicole made a face. She was so right there.

"Finding men has never been a problem for me," Venus offered up. "Keeping them? That's another story."

"The good ones or the so-so ones?"

Venus sighed. "Good or even so-so wouldn't be bad. Unfortunately, the only ones I seem to manage to hang onto are the creeps who cost you jobs or empty your bank accounts. Not the green-eyed dreamboats with chestnut hair and the kind of wicked, sexy grin that oughta be illegal."

Nicole got the definite impression that the "dreamboat" the barmaid referred to wasn't a work of fiction, but rather a reality. And she also guessed that he wasn't a part of the picture anymore.

Sydney made a knowing sound.

"What?"

"You got it bad, sister."

Nicole smiled. *You can say that again.*

Venus scowled. "Speak for yourself."

After Sydney admitted she was speaking for herself, Venus poured her another drink.

"We bad girls have it tough, you know?" Venus

said. "Those Goody Two-shoes have saying 'no' down to an art form, blaming morals or past hurts. We say yes, because of those same morals or past hurts! We just can't give up on the idea that the next handsome stud who comes along might erase what the last one did."

"Handsome studs are a dime a dozen."

Nicole sat up slightly as the barmaid named Venus approached. "Hey, girl, I almost forgot you were here. Come join us. Bad girls need to stick together."

Nicole squinted at both women, then pursed her lips. It wasn't so much Venus's straightforwardness that surprised her, but that she'd so correctly nailed her. Was it an innate gift, the ability to pick out those similar to you? Of course, in her case it wasn't all that difficult to tell which side of the good girl/bad girl equation she stood on, what with her tendency toward all black clothing—especially leather, all black clothing. Straight down to her thong.

But clothing or no, Nicole felt sure that despite their physical differences, she shared much in common with the other two women when it came to men and life in general. As for careers...well, no one said she had to tell them she was a professional thief and that she knew the worth of Sydney's gems right down to the carat weight.

She smiled wryly. "Bad girls. Are we forming a club here?"

Venus snorted. "Last club I belonged to was the Girl Scouts. I got kicked out when I was eleven." As Sydney raised a questioning brow, Venus explained. "Summer camp. I got caught sneaking into the boys' cabin to play Seven Minutes in Heaven. The troop leader came in just as I was heading into the closet with Tommy Callahan." She shook her head and sighed. "He had the cutest dimples. And cool braces."

Sydney nodded, wearing a similar look of reminiscence.

Nicole's amused smile widened into a grin. "I never made it past Brownies. I kept altering the uniform in a way that, well, didn't exactly meet with the troop leader's approval. But the boys liked it." She winked. "Besides, brown isn't my color." Of course, they didn't need to know that she'd also made off with the troop's petty cash box on the first day.

"Hell," Sydney proclaimed, "my mother never let me forget I got tossed outta preschool for showing the boys my underwear."

Venus snickered. "Hey, why was she complaining?"

"Yeah," Nicole said with a knowing look at Venus. They finished the thought in unison. "At least you were wearing 'em."

The three of them, strangers until ten minutes before, but sisters just the same, shared a moment of soft laughter. It had been a long time since Nicole had felt so connected to other women, and she enjoyed it. If only for a moment.

Venus said, "I guess we've been members of the bad girls' club since birth, huh?"

Sydney silently lifted her glass in salute, and Nicole followed suit. Venus popped the cap off a beer and joined them.

The door opened again, reminding Nicole what she was doing there. Two young women wearing business suits barely spared her and her new friends a glance as they joined the men in the booth.

"Oh, no, a good girl's in sight, reign in the lust," Venus whispered.

Nicole picked up her drink and moved next to Sydney, then introduced herself. They chatted for several more minutes, until the ring of Sydney's cell phone interrupted.

Venus moved away to wait on the two newcomers, then returned just as Sydney was finishing her call. The woman drained her glass and dropped a bill on the counter. Nicole noted the crisp one hundred dollar bill.

Venus picked it up. "I'll get your change."

Sydney told her to keep it and get Nicole good and drunk. Then, with a cheery wave, she walked toward the door. But before she could reach for the handle, the door opened and Nicole watched a man come in. She narrowed her eyes, taking in the big brown-haired man who had the solid build of a cop.

Number one weakness at ten o'clock. Her sexual radar homed in on him. Cop or no, he was a man. And a striking one at that.

She watched as he skirted around a departing Sydney, then approached the bar, his gaze on one woman and one woman only: Venus.

Nicole let out a long, mental sigh. It was just as well. After her last encounter with the opposite sex, she'd do well to fly solo for a while. Still, it could have been...interesting if the fine male specimen was the one shadowing her.

She eyed Venus, who looked a breath away from either blindsiding the latest arrival or pulling him across the bar and laying a wet one on him.

"Hi, Venus."

"What are you doing here?"

"I'm thirsty," he said as he slid onto a bar stool and tapped his fingers on the pitted wood surface of the bar. "What do you recommend? A Screaming Orgasm? Sex on the Beach?"

Venus smirked. "Screaming Orgasm Up Against the Wall is always a good choice."

"How about Screaming Orgasm Up Against the Bathroom Counter? Or in the Pool?" The man's grin was even dirtier than his words implied.

Nicole let out a low whistle, not having to question whether or not this was the man Venus had referred to earlier. "Yep. Definitely oughta be illegal." Just being within five feet of the couple reminded her why she could never swear off men, no matter how much trouble they caused. She smiled at Venus, then made her way out of the bar.

The door slowly closed behind her as she tucked her chin into her chest and scanned the street from beneath her lashes. Nothing. Not a single suspicious person in sight. Just an ordinary, perfect early summer day and the foot traffic it encouraged.

She shifted her backpack to her other shoulder as she started one way, then changed her mind and walked in the opposite direction, the sensation of being followed mysteriously gone.

Could she have been wrong? She took a deep breath, then released it, wondering if paranoia was something that went along with age. Of course, it didn't help that out of the three members of her family, she was the only active thief left. Her brother Jeremy had hung up the title a year ago when he'd met and married Joanna. Her father...

Nicole swallowed hard. Maybe that was why she

was so hypersensitive about everything lately. What had happened to her father...well, she was going to make damn sure it didn't happen to her.

She slid a glance over her shoulder. A shadow retreated into a doorway.

She twisted her lips. Maybe she hadn't been imagining things, after all....

ALEX CASSAVETES melded into the doorway of the pub the wily and alluring Nicole Bennett had exited moments earlier. He absently rubbed his chin. She'd spotted him. He knew she had. What did that say about him as a one-time detective in the N.Y.P.D. robbery division and current insurance investigator?

Apparently not a whole hell of a lot.

Alex pushed up his jacket sleeve and glanced at his watch. He'd be a moron to try to tail her now. He suspected she'd caught onto him before she'd even entered the pub. It's the reason he hadn't followed her in. He still couldn't believe that the instant he'd stepped out from the coffee shop where he'd been waiting across the street she'd looked back and made eye contact even though a good hundred feet separated them.

Damn.

Stepping from the doorway, he made his way in the opposite direction, not even looking at where Nicole had been moments before. To have come so far and to have blown it so close to meeting his objective was incompetent at best, stupid at worst.

The heels of his shoes thudded against the sidewalk, echoing against the building-crowded Baltimore street. Nicole Bennett, thief of thieves, had flown from New York to Baltimore a little more than three days ago.

And he'd been right there with her every step. Following her into lingerie shops. Eating lunch a few tables away from hers. Even securing the room across from hers in the glorified flophouse that advertised hourly rates on the faded brick exterior.

But nothing in his thirty-two-year existence had prepared him for meeting her gaze head-on.

"The eyes of a witch," Panayiota, his Greek grandmother would have said. Black, fathomless eyes that could either repel you or pull you in. He could only imagine what impact those almond-shaped eyes would have on him at close range. Photographs, no matter how vividly real, didn't come close to depicting the genuine article. He'd just learned that the hard way.

"You're losing it, Cassavetes," he muttered to himself, turning a corner and suppressing the urge to duck to the side and see if she was watching him.

No. His best bet now would be to return to the boardinghouse and hope she would come back so he could pick up her trail again.

Even as he thought it, Alex knew she wouldn't return. She was the type that, once she sensed danger, would disappear back into the woodwork from which she'd emerged. A search of her room yesterday and this morning had revealed absolutely nothing of the woman who inhabited it. Nothing that would require her to return to the room. His guess was that she either kept her personal items in her generously sized leather tote, or that her occasional visits to various bus and airport lockers explained the lack of anything left behind.

Which is exactly why she'd been so difficult to catch.

And precisely the reason he intended to catch her.

Alex Cassavetes always nabbed his man. Or in this case, his woman. A very clever, seductive and endlessly fascinating woman who slipped through his fingers like quicksilver and for the first time made him question his abilities as an insurance investigator.

He caught himself fingering an item in his pants pocket, then slid it out and stared at it. No, you wouldn't find Nicole Bennett's likeness on any Wanted posters. Or even any alerts circulating to local and federal law enforcement agencies. Nicole Bennett—if that was even her name—was smarter than that. For the most part, she targeted other thieves. Marks that would have to be the ultimate in obtuse to report the thefts. She was more of a ghost that sensed when a large score was about to go down and then would swoop in and make off with the booty with nary a soul the wiser.

Except for Alex.

He stepped into the lobby of the rundown hotel where he'd hung his hat for the past two days, eyed where an aging hooker and a john were haggling with the desk manager, then took the steps to the second floor two at a time.

He couldn't exactly pinpoint the moment when he'd put two-and-two together and come away with Nicole Bennett. He'd been in the middle of the third month of tracking down the diamonds that Christine Bowman and her dangerous band of thieves had made away with. Christine had been arrested and charged, and later convicted, of the theft and the death of two security guards, but the diamonds had never been recovered. The insurance company he worked for had been out a great deal of money. But something had been bothering him about the whole case, something hovering just beyond his reach. So he'd pulled an all-nighter going over everything related to the case when something in his brain finally clicked. He'd methodically thumbed through the security shots taken from a St. Louis bus station and found the image of the woman standing half in shadow in the far corner while Christine Bowman was arrested on the other side of the station. The mystery woman had gone unnoticed, despite her black leather trench coat and striking features. Then he'd rifled through photos taken from similar thefts, incidents where the thieves were caught but the spoils were curiously missing. And he'd come across two more partial photographs of the shadowy woman in black standing on the fringes of the goings-on. An interview with St. Louis P.I. Ripley Logan had yielded him a name: Nicole Bennett.

The same name on the hotel register for the room across from his.

He turned the corner of the second-floor hall. His room was halfway down the vomit-green corridor with its narrow wood doors and tarnished knob and lock plates. Room 107. He slid his key into the lock, then paused, the fine hairs on the back of his neck standing on end. He slid a glance over his shoulder at the peephole to Room 108. Nicole?

He pushed his door open and paused. Before he could question the wisdom of his actions, he walked across the hall and knocked on the door to Room 108, his gaze steadily on the peephole.

Silence.

Alex cocked a half grin. He knew she was there. Sensed it with every molecule.

He raised his hand to knock again, then heard the lock mechanism turn. And instantly found out exactly what it was like to encounter those coal-black eyes up close and personal.

Nicole Bennett swung the door open all the way, then leaned against the jamb and crossed her arms.

Alex felt like someone had just given him a sucker punch to the gut. There emanated such a sizzling current about her that he was distantly surprised he wasn't suffering electrocution.

"You wanted something?" she asked, looking at him as intently as he was looking at her.

Alex's grin grew. Oh, but she was slick. Very slick. You wouldn't suspect that she was aware he was tailing her. But he knew. Knew by the way he hadn't heard her step to the door—she must have been standing on the other side of it watching for him. And since he knew she'd already seen him on the street, well, he had plenty of evidence that proved she wasn't that dumb.

He allowed his gaze to drop to the deep vee of her black leather vest. She had a knockout figure. Not that you could tell by the loose leather coat she'd worn up until a few weeks ago when the warm weather had forbidden it. He appreciated the subtle muscle tone of her arms, and the way her breasts pressed together, offering up a virtual buffet of sweet flesh that made his mouth water.

"Yes," he said, raising his gaze back to her face to find her cheeks touched with the slightest color.

"Hi, I'm Alex." He waited for her to offer an introduction of herself, but wasn't surprised when she didn't. "I'm across the hall." He tried looking into her room, as if he hadn't been in it two minutes after she had left that morning. "Did housekeeping bring you towels? Because I—"

She stepped from the door to the tiny bathroom to her right and grabbed a dingy gray, threadbare towel. She handed it to him.

"Thanks."

"Don't mention it." She closed the door, then slid the lock home.

Alex stood for long moments grinning at his feet. There hadn't been the sound of her moving away from the door, which meant that she was probably looking at him again from the peephole. He decided it wouldn't be a good idea to give a little salute as he crossed back to the other side of the hall.

Interesting. He let himself into his room. She had not only come back to the hotel, but didn't seem fazed in the least by the knowledge that he was tailing her. Or she wasn't entirely certain and was trying to force his hand. Either way, he gave her a lot of credit. Never in his career had he met a woman so sure of herself.

And so totally hot.

Maybe this wasn't over yet.

2

ALEX.

Mmm...

Nicole stood on the fringes of the party, her short, sleek socialite blond wig in place—nothing too flashy or too trendy—her black dress clingy yet elegant. Her second favorite quote after Bette Davis's memorable words were "Lead me not into temptation; I can find the way myself," written by author Rita Mae Brown. And if Alex was anything, he was one hundred percent pure temptation. And like it or not, she was definitely leading herself into it...and to him.

She twisted her lips and scanned the gathering of a hundred and fifty people looking for anyone that might appear out of place. A little voice told her that the instant she'd made her tail, she should have been in a taxi straight to the airport. Forget the boardinghouse. Forget the job. Forget everything but losing Alex. She accepted a champagne flute from a passing waiter with a small, close-lipped smile, then watched him move on, unwittingly comparing him to the man who was occupying far too much of her thoughts.

Alex.

At over six feet, he was tall enough to put him squarely in the danger category when it came to her and her attraction to tall men. His hair was nearly as dark as hers, brown and silky and enticingly touchable. His eyes were an opaque green and seemed to crackle with a knowing, a sexual energy that made her mouth water just looking at him. But it was his lips—full and captivating—that made her nipples tighten and her thighs vibrate.

Okay, so he was attractive. To the point of distraction. Which was exactly the reason she should never have gone back to the hotel. Especially since his very essence seemed to scream "cop." Hadn't she had enough problems in her love life lately without adding a sex god of a cop to the mix?

She wrinkled her nose and lifted her glass to toast an elderly gentleman eyeing her favorably from across the room. A good six hours had passed since she'd first spotted Alex, then watched him unlock the door across the hall. Of course, she'd had no idea he would turn and look right at her through the peephole, then be even bolder yet by knocking on her door and asking about housekeeping when he hadn't even walked fully into his room first. But at least her suspicions had been confirmed.

She pretended to sip the sparkling wine. Definitely Dom Perignon. The Theismans of the Baltimore Theismans, the multimillion-dollar hosts of tonight's little soiree, knew how to throw a party. Nothing but the best, especially for the first-year wedding anniversary of the mismatched couple standing near the fireplace mantel. Nicole slightly craned her neck, judging Mrs. Theisman to be closer to twenty than she was thirty, and Mr. Theisman, head of Theisman Telecommunications, pushing closer to seventy. She idly wondered what place number this particular trophy wife held.

Two? No. More than likely three. Or possibly even four.

Nicole politely nodded at a woman who came to stand near her.

"Lovely couple, aren't they?" the guest commented.

Nicole hiked a brow. "Lovely" wasn't a word she'd use to describe the twosome. Revolting hit closer to home. "Aren't they just?" she said before discreetly moving away.

She shifted her weight from one expensive pump to the other. Who was she to criticize? If she judged the men she dated more on character than looks, maybe she wouldn't run into the problems she did. Perhaps if she expanded her criteria beyond tall, gorgeous and built like a linebacker, she wouldn't have to worry about waking up one morning and finding the guy had come across her stolen Tiffany jewelry and called the cops on her.

A waitress drifted by her from the opposite direction. Nicole squinted at her neck where the top of a black tattoo peeked from her starched white shirt. If her calculations were correct, the thieves were going to strike tonight, taking full advantage of the hubbub created by the party, when the house's security system would be on low alert and it would be easy for the thieves to move among the guests. They would also probably fall back on the tried and true method of posing as temporary catering staff in order to do it. Not difficult considering the young Mrs. Theisman had chosen a new caterer with a transient, unbonded staff instead of going with the long-established company her peers used. No doubt attempting to make her mark as a stylish hostess. Instead she'd set herself up as an easy target.

Nicole's gaze went to the sweeping staircase to her left. She'd gotten wind of the heist the day before Sebastian had elected himself her latest ex. She didn't know the details, or who was in on it, but once word started circulating in her circles about easily fenced merchandise, the theft was as good as done. Since then, she'd had three days to do her homework. She knew there were three safes in the eight-bedroom Theisman mansion. One in the downstairs study. One in the master bathroom. And another cleverly hidden beneath the oriental carpet under a double bed in the third guest room.

She guessed that would be the hiding place of the over two hundred thousand in insured uncut rubies Mr. Theisman had bought as an anniversary gift for his trophy wife.

The question was whether the thieves had hit the safe yet.

She glanced at her slender faux-diamond watch, then accidentally spilled a bit of champagne on the front of her dress. Excusing herself from the small group of guests that conversed around her, she headed for the back of the house and the kitchen, rather than seeking out the bathroom just off the foyer. Within minutes she had her shoes in her hand and was slinking up the back stairwell, easily navigating the frenzied catering staff in the kitchen, and surmising that at least one of the original servers was missing. Her observation was immediately confirmed by the woman sweating over an oven when she asked if anyone had seen a man named Mike.

Nicole reached the second floor, thankful for vain wealthy homeowners who didn't like to see the help unless they had to. She had access to every room upstairs without the risk of being seen. Dim, recessed lighting illuminated the long, curving hall bearing gold-framed prints of Baltimore. Worlds away from the water-stained dingy corridors of the Commodore Hotel. But somehow Nicole always felt safer in those dingy places. More...real, somehow. Less exposed. Although she'd long ago learned to blend in with any crowd, it took less effort to disappear into the background of the less privileged. The people who knew what it meant to struggle. They weren't struggling to make a towering mortgage or work a sauna into their monthly budget. No, they were struggling for survival. And rarely looked beyond the few inches in front of them because they hoped somewhere there lay their salvation, the answer to all their problems.

Alex intruded on her thoughts again. He'd find it difficult to blend in anywhere. Aside from his considerable height and striking good looks, there was something...different about him, something Nicole couldn't put her finger on. Something that bothered her on a fundamental level and had nothing to do with his likely being a cop. Something that made her want to return to the hotel that night instead of getting on the twelve o'clock train back to New York.

With the rubies, she thought, forcefully reminding herself of the reason she was there.

She ducked into the guest room across the hall from the one that held the third safe and pushed the door closed until it was just slightly ajar.

How long had it been since her mind had been on

anything but the task at hand? If she had been considering which law enforcement agency Alex worked for, that would be one thing. Wondering what it would be like to run her tongue along the fine, freshly shaven line of his strong jaw was quite another.

A shadow.

Nicole reached for her purse with her left hand and took out the small-caliber pistol there. The only time that the saying "size doesn't matter" applied was in the world of guns. As long as the wielder knew what she was doing, a peashooter was more than enough firepower to stop a stampede of bison. She thumbed the safety and watched a figure in a waiter's uniform exit the master bedroom at the end of the hall, then move in her direction. She made a face. Either he was greedy and had gone after what trinkets the main safe held, or he hadn't figured out that the rubies were most likely in the third safe. Which made him either wet behind the ears or a moron. Or a dangerous combination of both. While she could easily explain away her presence in the guest room—that very notably didn't hold a safe—by saying she'd felt light-headed and needed to lie down for a moment, a man wearing a waiter's uniform sneaking into the guest bedroom that did hold a safe was another matter altogether.

"And, lucky contestant, would you like to see the prize you'll be playing for?" she murmured to herself. "Roddy, show him what he could win tonight...."

And that prize was what she fully planned to take away from him the instant he had the little beauties in hand and had successfully made his escape.

The thief glanced in her direction. Nicole moved back a couple of inches to keep from being seen.

And found her backside flush against something very hard, very warm and very definitely male.

"Oh!" She gasped, feeling every panic alarm go off all at once.

"MMM. THE CONTESTANT'S very lucky, indeed," Alex murmured against Nicole's ear.

The scent of cinnamon candy, subtle yet distinctive, teased his nose, while certain strategic areas teased other parts of his anatomy.

Damn, but she smelled good. Clean, spicy and over-whelmingly sexy. Alex couldn't resist resting his chin against the hair curving against the side of Nicole's neck as he steadied her with his hands on her hips.

"Seems we keep bumping into each other," she said, her voice barely above a whisper. The touch of nerves humming just below the surface made it sound like a purr. He idly wondered if she might be part cat. Such feline characteristics would be an advantage in her chosen profession. One had to be light on her feet to be successful in this business. And, of course, it didn't hurt to have an extra life or two in case you lost one along the way.

He skimmed his fingers down her bare arm, feeling her shiver against him as he eased the small, custom-ized pistol she held from her warm fingers. He looked at it. "Cute."

He heard her swallow. "Effective."

He chuckled quietly, keeping in mind that the other thief they were watching thought he was alone on the second floor. "Only if you draw a bead on your oppo-nent before he draws one on you."

"Mmm. Yes, that does help."

Was it possible she'd sensed his identity straight off? Or was it the sound of his voice that had given him away? Either way, he was pretty sure she knew who he was.

He also noticed that she was regaining her composure with each second that passed. He slid the palm-size gun into his tux jacket. She wriggled to free herself from the grasp of his other hand.

"Shh." He tightened his hold on her hip, then pressed his mouth against her ear. "Hold still or we'll miss the show."

Alex watched over her shoulder as the thief entered the third guest bedroom and closed the door after himself.

For long moments he stood still, listening to Nicole's uneven breathing, taking in her unique scent, and wondering where in the hell she'd gotten the blond wig. It had taken him a full minute to realize that it was her after her transformation. She'd disappeared into a restaurant bathroom then emerged a short time later looking like she did now, her usual attire presumably tucked into her black tote. A tote she'd cleverly hidden in the bushes of a neighboring house before joining the Theisman party.

"The show appears to be over," she murmured.

Alex slowly blinked, realizing he had yet to release her. And that she had yet to make another move to free herself. "Depends on which show you're referring to."

He glanced down at the pale expanse of shoulder left bare by her black dress. The moonlight streaming in through the window kissed her skin, making it glow dimly while the rest was cloaked in shadow.

"How long do you give him?" he asked, drawing the

back of his index finger up her arm. She didn't shiver this time, but she did shift, moving until her hot little bottom pressed more insistently against the front of his slacks. He sensed the move was far from accidental.

"If he's good, five minutes."

"And if he's not?"

"Enough time to hang himself."

Alex grinned. "Of course it helps when the lady of the manor gives you the combination to the safe."

Nicole stepped away then faced him, staring at him in the dark.

"Ah, didn't figure that one out, huh?" Alex tried to ignore the way his body missed her heat. "I caught our friend having a little chat with the very young Mrs. Theisman out back."

"Maybe she was complaining about the paté."

He dropped his gaze to the vee of her bodice, then down farther to where the hem hugged her legs. With those gorgeous gams he wondered why she always hid them under all that black leather. "If she was, then she was giving him a mouth-to-mouth taste of it."

"Hmm. Interesting."

"No. Predictable."

"I didn't see it."

"Now that is interesting," he commented.

Nicole seemed to consider the shoes she still held in one hand.

"So when were you planning on snatching the loot?"

He caught a glimmer of humor in her eyes. "Snatch the loot?"

"Grab the goods. Steal the stash. Rob the robber?"

She tucked a strand of the platinum-blond wig behind her ear. "New York. Queens. Robbery/homicide."

He grimaced as she stepped a short way away.

"Excuse me?" he asked.

She held his gaze. "That's where you're from, right? Queens?"

Oh, she was good. Almost too good. And downright dangerous. As well as provocatively sexy, which made her even more dangerous. He'd do well to remember that.

She twisted her lips. "What I can't get is what you're doing here."

Alex crossed his arms, as much to keep from touching her as in a defensive maneuver. "Astoria. Insurance investigator."

"Mmm. Maybe now. But you used to be a cop, right?"

"Detective."

"That's what I thought." She turned back toward the door to look out the crack. "And Astoria is Queens."

Alex's gaze dropped to her pert bottom and the way it jutted out just slightly as she inclined to look into the hall. He stifled a groan. A stubbornly clever woman with a killer body. He felt the weight of the pistol in his pocket. She was also a felon that he should be arresting.

"Are you here to guard the Theismans' insured property?" she asked in that husky whisper that felt like the caress of a woman's fingers.

"No, I'm watching you."

She turned from the door again to look at him.

He couldn't resist a grin. "Surprised you."

"Yes...you could say that."

"I just did."

He caught her smile before she reached down and began putting her shoes back on one by one.

"Where are you going?"

"Leaving."

"Going to position yourself to ambush the thief?"

She gently shook her head. "No, I think I'll call this one a bust and go home."

"Not because of me, I hope."

She smiled.

"And here I thought you'd stick around at least long enough to find out what I'm really doing here."

A creak of a door.

They both swung to watch the thief exit the guest room across the hall. He clutched a black velvet bag in his hand. But rather than making a run for it, his attention was on another door. Namely the one Alex and Nicole stood behind.

Alex eyed the woman standing in front of him. He hadn't known how much he had been hoping for just such an opportunity until he hauled one very wily, supremely sexy Nicole Bennett into his arms. She stared up at him in naked shock. Then he slowly lowered his mouth to hers and kissed her, absently thinking that she tasted like cinnamon candy, too.

3

SO...TALL. SO...HARD. SO...HOT.

And far too slow.

Nicole kept her eyelids cracked open, watching Alex's finely honed features as he launched a mock attack on her mouth. Only there was nothing mock about her instant reaction to it. She heard the door creak farther open behind her, but immediately forgot about it as Alex moved his hand up the outside of her leg then slid his fingertips under the hem of her skirt. She dipped her tongue into his mouth just as he found out that she had absolutely nothing on underneath the classy shift. She drank in his expression of first shock, then pure wicked pleasure. Ah. Just her type. The kind of guy capable of compensating for any surprise thrown his way. That assessment was quickly confirmed when he traced the line of her clean-shaven pubis.

Nicole's knees buckled at the rush of instant and overpowering heat caused by his intimate touch. All the while, his mouth continued to slowly explore hers.

Too slowly.

Deciding to ratchet things up a notch, she tunneled her fingers wildly through his hair then pushed her mouth almost painfully against his, swirling her tongue against his teeth like a starving woman. She was rewarded with a small groan...and the feel of his hand circling around to her bare bottom where he clutched her roughly to his growing hardness.

Mmm. The long, thick ridge she felt under his trousers felt...promising. She wiggled her hips to get a better sense, then smiled as she recklessly kissed him. Very promising, indeed.

Things escalated very quickly. One moment Nicole was trying to speed things up, the next she was dizzy from the quick pace. She forgot about the house, the jewels, the thief that could still be watching them. She tunneled her fingers into the front of Alex's slacks, desperately needing to touch the silken length of him. The only thing she knew was the accumulating need to go as far as she dared with this man—a man with the power to put her behind bars, yet who set her on fire with a simple, well-placed touch.

Alex caught her fingers just as she touched his hard heat, then broke free from their spiraling kiss.

"I...think he's gone," he said raggedly, his breathing irregular, his hair gorgeously tousled from where she'd restlessly played with and tugged on it.

"Who?" she whispered, blinking as her gaze traveled from his hair to his eyes then his decidedly decadent mouth.

"Who, indeed," he said, his eyes darkening.

Nicole gasped when he shoved her against the opposite wall, then followed, sandwiching her between the wall and his heat. A picture frame tipped back and forth and a chair toppled over as Alex kicked it out of the way, then sweet heaven descended as he picked her up and wrapped her legs around his hips, pressing his hard arousal against her soft, exposed flesh.

Nicole had always gotten a rush out of stealing. And

she couldn't remember a time when she didn't love sex. But when the two of them crashed together, it nearly sent her plummeting right over the edge. She couldn't seem to get enough of Alex fast enough. She pulled at his tie, shoved his suit coat down over his arms, then dove for his belt buckle and the zipper beyond. She heard the ripping of material. Namely that of the strap of her dress where Alex was trying to gain access to her breasts. She smiled at him through their kiss.

"Sorry," he rasped.

Nicole ripped open his shirt, sending buttons ricocheting around the room. "Not a problem."

She took in the wide, hard planes of his chest. No donut-induced middle about this ex-cop. He was a pure, undiluted hottie with a chest that could make a grown woman cry. She pressed her palms flat against his nipples, then dragged her fingers down over his taut, rippled flesh. Damn. She hadn't seen a guy this hot since she'd dated the captain of the football team back in high school. Maybe she'd been going after the wrong guys. Maybe the jocks were where it was at.

She gave a soft laugh at the twisted thought even as she wriggled her hips to get the room she needed to free his erection. She finally held his long, hard length in her fingers. Impressive. Very impressive, indeed. She'd heard of extralarge condoms being available, but had never actually had the cause to buy one.

Speaking of condoms...

Alex fastened his mouth over her right breast, chasing the air from her lungs and causing her to throw her head back against the wall and groan. God, but he had a great mouth. Tiny tendrils of fire licked along her nerve endings, ending in a throbbing pool of molten electricity right between her thighs.

"Rubber," she said breathlessly. "Give me a rubber."

Alex froze.

Just froze.

His mouth still rested against her breast.

His erection still pulsed against her too hot flesh.

But he wasn't moving anymore.

And Nicole didn't want to know the reason why.

He finally pulled back enough to look into her face. She didn't have to ask. The answer was right there in his tortured expression.

Nicole felt the tremendous urge to hit him.

"You've got to be shitting me," she whispered, uncrossing her ankles behind his back and sliding her feet down to stand on her own. "You don't have a rubber?"

"The tux is a rental."

"Your wallet?"

"Contains my ID and cash."

"No condom."

He shook his head, looking as frustrated as she felt. "No condom."

Nicole sagged against the wall, feeling the incredible, confusing urge to cry as sexual frustration pressed from the inside out. She wanted release. But for her there was only one way that would really do it for her. And that was feeling Alex deep inside her. Oral sex wouldn't do. Petting, no matter how heavy, could never lessen the need.

She swallowed hard, just then realizing that Alex was staring as hardly at her as she was at him.

"Wait a minute," she whispered, looking toward the large bed they had purposely avoided.

She brushed by Alex, the tips of her breasts rubbing against his wide chest as she made her way to the nightstand to the right of the bed. She opened and closed the three drawers there, then rounded the bed and checked the drawers on the other side.

No condoms.

What kind of hosts were the Theismans, anyway?

She felt Alex's heat against her back where she stood staring at the nightstand. She wanted to scream with the frustration of it all. Until she felt something cold encircle her left wrist, then heard the unmistakable sound of metal teeth ratcheting against each other.

"Sorry," Alex said into her ear. "But once I say what I have to, I think you'll understand."

Handcuffs.

Nicole turned and watched as he fastened the other side of the handcuffs to his right wrist. Not to the bedpost.

Not that it made a difference. Without a condom, sex was out of the question. She loved sex, and seriously wanted to indulge in some major mind-blowing sex with Alex, but she wasn't stupid. Intimacy without a rubber was like playing Russian roulette with half the chambers filled.

She collapsed to sit on the mattress and sighed. "You don't have a condom, but you have handcuffs," she said absently, considering the heavy metal weighing down her wrist.

She blinked up at him. "You seriously need to re-evaluate your priorities, man."

He chuckled softly then took out his cell phone and called a taxi.

"Where are you taking me?" Nicole was afraid he was going to say the nearest police station. Although she knew that he had nothing on her, and she certainly didn't have any stolen goods on her person, that didn't mean he didn't intend to have her arrested. After all, he still had to tell her what he was doing watching her.

He slid the phone back into his inside jacket pocket. "Home."

FIVE HOURS and a plane trip later, Alex cursed his decision not to stop at the nearest drug store to stock up on, um, certain supplies before taking Nicole to his recently and very roughly renovated loft in lower Manhattan. Just seeing Nicole handcuffed to the headboard of his old iron bed made him hard as a rock, despite the majorly annoyed expression on her face as she tried to cross her arms over her chest but could only cross one. A loud thwap sounded when she slapped her free hand against the mattress. "This really stinks, you know."

Didn't it just.

Never had been the time that Alex had regretted who he was. But in that one moment, he'd have given his pension not to be an insurance investigator. Instead he wished he was a regular guy free to do what he would with the walking sexpot looking at him with barely contained rage.

Then again, if he were a regular guy with no professional interest in Nicole, he wouldn't be standing where he was, either, essentially having kidnapped Nicole Bennett. If anyone knew the repercussions of his actions, he did, no matter how desperate he was for her help. Although he sensed Nicole would be the last one to press charges.

He hated catch-22s. The problem was that lately life had turned into one huge catch-22 for him.

Standing at the end of the bed, he dragged toward him Nicole's ever-present black leather backpack, which he'd retrieved from the Theisman's neighbor's shrubs before leaving the wealthy Baltimore subdivision in a taxi.

Nicole sighed and rolled her eyes to stare at the ceiling.

Alex ignored the stretch of elegant neck she presented him with, and the way one side of her dress dipped dangerously low from where he'd torn the strap. He looked down at where he was pulling items out of the pack. A small bag of toiletries. Black leather pants, vest, coat and boots and...God was that a leather thong? He let the scrap of material hang from his index finger and decided that it must be. He looked at her. She glared back.

"Interesting."

"Yeah, well, I'm sure I could find an interesting item of clothing or two if I went through your stuff, too."

He checked the empty bag. "No pajamas?"

She hiked a brow. "You're holding them."

Alex let the thong drop to the bed.

His gaze slid up to where she had her long, long legs crossed at the ankles on the bed, lingering around the hemline and the bare area in question just beyond.

Oh, boy. This wasn't going exactly the way he planned.

He stuffed her things back into her bag then tossed it

to a nearby chair. Moments later, he threw a pair of lightweight summer pajamas to her from his top drawer.

Nicole picked them up. "Are these for me or you?"

"Both," he muttered under his breath, thinking he should have cuffed her to the dormant radiator. "You."

"They still have the tags on them."

That was because his mother had bought them for him and, like Nicole, he wasn't much of a pajama man.

"They're new," he told her. "Put them on."

She tossed them to lay on top of her bag across the room. He had to give her credit for her aim. "I'm not doing anything until you tell me what's going on."

Alex grinned. There it was. The demand he'd been waiting for since he'd snapped the cuffs on her in Maryland.

Throughout the two taxi rides and a plane flight back to New York, he had waited for Nicole to ask the question. She hadn't, of course. Instead she'd sat like a she-cat, alternately glaring at him then licking her lips in a way that made him forget his own name, much less what his objective was.

And his objective was very simple.

He crossed his arms over his chest and stared at her across the foot of the bed. "I need you to help me catch Dark Man."

She squinted at him with those unsettling eyes, then snapped her mouth shut, trying again to cross her arms over her chest, causing the cuffs to rattle.

He didn't have to explain who Dark Man was. Most thieves, once they reached a certain level of success and notoriety, were known by nicknames. He absently rubbed his chin. He'd taken to calling Nicole Black Cat. Some other names included Pablo, for the English thief who stole strictly Picassos, and there was even a Mr. Ed, who concentrated his extracurricular activities on rustling highly insured thoroughbred racehorses.

Bestowing the nickname Dark Man, however, hadn't been done in a light or amusing way. Dark Man was named as such because he was utterly and totally dark. When he was involved in a theft, people usually ended up hurt. Or dead.

And no one seemed to know who he was.

Alex went on. "Two months ago he was involved in the Norton Museum job in Omaha. Two security guards and an assistant curator—who was father to twin two-year-old boys—were shot dead at point-blank range."

Nicole stared at where she was running her palm along the length of her skirt then back again. Stress lines bracketed the sides of her naughty mouth, but otherwise he couldn't tell how she was taking what he was saying.

"Three months before that, there was the gallery job in San Francisco. Four injured, one paralyzed for life."

He rounded the bed and sat down next to her on the mattress. "I want this guy, Nicole. I want him so bad I can't think straight."

She blinked to stare at him, her dark eyes questioning. "I thought you weren't a cop anymore."

"I'm not," he said, but didn't offer anything more. She didn't have to know that Dark Man had haunted him throughout his career. Or that the thief was responsible for twenty-five percent of the policy payouts issued by his company last year.

"And I should help you...why?" she asked.

Because it's the right thing to do, he wanted to say.

But he didn't. Because if there was one thing he'd learned during his career in the N.Y.P.D., it was that right and wrong were twisted in the criminal underworld. Black became white and the gray area stretched to a point where even the black and white were essentially obliterated.

"Because if you don't, then I turn you over to the authorities investigating the Bowman diamond heist last summer."

He had to give her credit—she didn't even blink. "I wasn't involved with it."

He gave her a half smile. "After I get done explaining everything to the authorities, do you really think it will matter?"

He watched her slender throat work around a swallow. Alex decided he liked the blond wig. It was short and sassy and showed her neck and shoulders off in a sexily elegant way.

Nicole said, "I can't help you."

"Why?"

She slanted a gaze in his direction as if addressing a particularly slow child. "The code."

"Ah," he said, narrowing his eyes. "You mean honor among thieves and all that."

She smiled at him, but there was little or no amusement in the action. "Something like that."

"And what do you think your fellow thieves would think of you targeting them for theft, then leaving them alone to take the fall?"

Color flushed her cheeks as she cursed under her breath. "You wouldn't dare."

At this point, Alex would.

Dark Man had plagued him throughout his eight-year career with the N.Y.P.D. He even suspected that the thief's first known job at a small folk art museum in SoHo had coincided with Alex's first day on the job in robbery/homicide.

But it wasn't just that Dark Man was a thorn in his side, or that Alex wanted to settle a score like you see in those macho "B" movies or dime-store novels.

No. He needed to get him because he was no longer a harmless thief. He was a serial killer who seemed to enjoy taking people's lives more than the loot.

And no one, nowhere, had a clue as to his real identity.

Oh, sure, the police had worked up a psychological profile on him. Mid-thirties. Loner. Classic passive-aggressive with sociopathic tendencies. But Alex could have told you that just reading the crime reports. The thief taunted his victims before killing them. Goaded them into risking their lives for material objects, then appeared to take great joy in making them pay for such a shallow move.

But the police profiler had also said that Dark Man would be a good-looking man. Popular with the ladies. Perhaps even a man well known in the public sector.

Did Nicole know him?

Alex discovered that during his thought processes he'd placed his hand on her bare knee and was lightly tracing circles on her pale skin with his thumb. If she did know who Dark Man was, he knew straight-out asking her wouldn't get the intended results.

But forcing her to work with him...well, that was an altogether different tack that he hoped would yield him the man he'd been searching for so long. His determination had little to do with the fact that the insurance company had paid out a great deal of money to cover the items he'd stolen. It had everything to do with his belief that the only room the guy was entitled to inhabit was an eight-by-eight prison cell for the rest of his unnatural life.

Alex raised his eyes to look into Nicole's, only she was watching his thumb make those lazy circles.

He removed his hand.

She moved her leg out of the way, then reached up to draw the blond wig from her head. Alex watched, fascinated, as she removed one, then two pins and her silky dark hair swept down to frame her pale face, in one blink taking her from icy cold temptress to dangerously sexy seductress.

"How do you think I can help you?"

Risky question, that, he thought as his gaze dropped to where her dark hair teased her nipples through the thin black fabric of her dress. His mouth watered just remembering the tangy taste of her skin. Her instant, uninhibited response.

Had he ever been with a woman so spontaneous? A woman who knew straight off what she wanted, no game-playing, no wondering if it was too soon or if she would look too bad if she revealed she wanted him as badly as he wanted her?

Oh, and Alex definitely wanted Nicole. Just like a sinner who couldn't help but sin.

He got up from the bed and held out his hand. She instantly dropped the two hairpins into his palm.

"You have the uncanny ability to know when something's going to happen before it does," he told her.

The cuffs clanked against the iron headboard as she propped the wig on one of the two iron posts. "How long, exactly, have you been watching me?"

Alex pocketed the pins, then picked up the pajamas and refolded them, thinking of the countless photographs of her that covered the corkboard in his office at work. "Long enough."

"Mmm." He watched her recross her legs in a slow, languid way designed to drive any man mad. "And did it make you...hot? You know, watching me when I didn't know you were?"

Alex couldn't seem to take his gaze away from her slender thighs, still hearing the sound of skin sliding against skin.

"You know, watching me, but not being able to touch me?"

Alex forced his gaze up to her face. "My surveillance was of a strictly professional nature."

She considered him for a long moment, then held up the hand bearing the metal shackles. "And I take it this is a new addition to the insurance investigator's handbook?"

Alex cracked a grin.

She shook her head, appearing to fight her own smile. "You're a naughty, naughty boy, Alex..."

"Cassavetes," he offered.

Her eyes narrowed slightly, then she relaxed. "Cassavetes. I should have guessed when you told me Astoria. Greek, right?"

He ran his hand through his hair then sighed. "You couldn't be more Greek unless you lived in Greece."

He wasn't exactly sure why he'd offered up that little bit of information as he placed the folded pajamas
next to her again.

His family, immediate and extended, seemed to exist in a sort of isolated cultural vacuum. His parents
had moved to New York from the Peloponnese right
after he was born, bringing his father's widowed
mother with them. Then five years later, his mother's
two brothers and a female cousin had come over, as
well. His grandmother, right up until she had died a
couple years ago, had never learned to communicate in
English. And almost all of his uncle's shoe repair business was conducted in Greek.

Of course, he and his younger sister, Athena, were
the only ones in the family to dare venture beyond the
borough boundaries, Alex to work in a precinct in
lower Manhattan, Athena to work in a restaurant in
Little Italy, committing the worst of all crimes by not
only rejecting her own heritage, but seeming to adopt
that of another country.

What went unsaid was that they were already living
under the flag of yet another country.

Strangely, though, his family was proud of their
Greek-American heritage and dedicatedly displayed
both flags outside both their house and at their corner
supermarket in Astoria.

Nicole cleared her throat. "You know, I've always
wondered...how do you say 'sex' in Greek?"

He bet she'd always wondered. More likely, she was
looking for a way to throw him off track. And it was
working. "Sex."

She laughed. "No. Seriously."

"I am serious."

She considered him for a long moment. "Okay, then. Although it's not much a part of my vocabulary...what about 'love'?"

"*Agapee*," he said automatically.

He reached for the throw at the foot of the bed and moved it so she could get it if she wanted without risking injury.

"I thought we'd get some sleep first," he said, glancing at his watch to find it after 2:00 a.m. "Then we can get a fresh start in the morning."

"I haven't agreed to anything yet."

He gestured toward the cuffs. "You will."

"Confident. I like that in a man."

Sexy. He liked that in a woman.

Nicole watched him move around the large open area of the loft, taking an extra top sheet from a set of drawers, and a pillow from the other side of the bed, then heading for the couch a good twenty feet away but still with a clear sight of the bed.

The cuffs clanked again. "You, um, wouldn't have any condoms in those drawers over there, would you?" she asked quietly.

Alex grinned as he made up the couch, then stretched out to lay across it in his newly rented tux slacks and shirt. "Nope."

Her long-suffering sigh filled the high-ceilinged area. "Some sex life you must have."

"Who says I don't go through a case of them a month and that I just ran out last night?" he asked.

He waited for her response, thinking she looked all too tempting there, handcuffed to his bed.

There was a twenty-four-hour convenience store on the corner....

"I say," she whispered, then scooted down and rolled to her side.

Unfortunately, she was right.

Alex lay staring at the ceiling some twenty-five feet above him, thinking not for the first time that he should paint the black beams white or beige or something. Open the place up a bit.

But the diversionary tactic didn't work. Because all he could think about was how long the night was going to be without sleep. And the reason he wasn't going to be able to sleep was that there was a red-hot sexy woman lying in his bed and not only did she appear to want him in it with her, but he wanted more than anything to be in it with her.

Oh, he definitely had not thought this plan through. Because if he had, he would have not only bought a box of condoms, he would have invested in the damn company that made them.

4

ALEX GROANED and tried to snag the sexy, ghostly image haunting his dream. Nicole Bennett. He had not only apprehended her, but had finally put into action his plan to entice her to help him. But she had this strange blond wig on...and was wearing his pajamas. Well, "wearing" wasn't quite accurate. Partially wearing them was closer. She'd only buttoned the top button, letting the flaps fall on either side of her toned abdomen, and she'd rolled the tops of the pants down dangerously low so that pale, taut skin taunted and teased and her navel ring winked at him as she moved. With a smoldering, provocative look, she kept tempting him closer. He moved the top flap of the pajama shirt aside and laved her large nipples with his tongue, and then tunneled his fingers into the back of the pants and molded her sweet bottom with his fingers...only to have her move away and waggle her finger at him teasingly, reminding him that he couldn't have her.

Alex awakened with a start, surprised to find his breathing ragged, his member rock hard and his heart hammering.

Good God, what had that been about?

He ran his hands through his hair again and again, trying to get a grip on his runaway thoughts.

Condoms, he realized. The damn dream had been about the lack of available condoms.

He jackknifed upright on the sofa, then planted his bare feet firmly on the pitted wood planks of his floor, waiting for his vision to clear. Slowly he registered that sunlight was streaming through the tall multipane windows that ran the length of the wall to his left...and that his apartment was strangely silent.

He jerked his head up to stare at the bed across the room, then catapulted from the sofa.

Empty.

The covers were pushed aside, the handcuffs left hanging open on the iron bar where he'd fastened one cuff.

Of course last night the other cuff had been firmly attached to Nicole Bennett's wrist.

"Damn," he muttered, striding across the room. Her bag was gone along with her. He picked up the blanket. Also gone were his pajamas.

What did she want with his pajamas?

And just how in the hell had she gotten out of the cuffs?

He checked his pocket for the hairpins. No, she hadn't managed to get them out somehow. There they still were. But obviously she hadn't needed them to free herself. That explained why she'd given them up so readily.

He smacked the pins against the night table then stalked to the bathroom. He saw to his morning ritual of brushing his teeth, washing his face and applying deodorant by rote, then changed out of the tux and into a pair of jeans and black T-shirt. He stared at the T-shirt in the mirror, then yanked it off, replacing it with a red one. Black reminded him too much of the damn woman who had slipped through his fingers yet again.

Only this time she knew not only who he was and what he wanted, but where he lived.

Damn, damn, damn.

The telephone rang.

Alex stepped toward the kitchen—little more than a stretch of counters with a sink flanked by a refrigerator and stove against the far wall—and snatched up the cordless receiver.

"Hey," he said gruffly. Coffee. He needed coffee, he thought, staring at the ancient coffeepot a few feet away.

"*Kalimera*," his mother said—"good morning" in Greek. "Is that any way to answer your phone?"

Not Nicole.

Alex's shoulders slumped as he looked at his watch. It was after nine. Since he'd finally dropped off to sleep at somewhere around five, that meant Nicole could be virtually anywhere east of the Mississippi, on her way to anywhere beyond that point. And he was completely clueless as to where to look for her first. Now that she knew he'd been following her, finding her at any of her regular hangouts was a no go.

The thought that she could virtually disappear from the face of the earth made his throat tighten.

He hadn't realized he'd let rip a series of curse words in Greek until his mother asked, "What is it, *agapemou*, my love?"

"Nothing," he muttered. "Look, Ma, can I call you back?"

Like sometime next week when he had his shit back together?

"Actually, this is more than a courtesy call, Alexanthros," she said. "Your sister...she's gone."

Again? he thought but didn't say.

He really couldn't deal with this right now. Not when someone else was noticeably missing.

"Your father and I are worried sick. She went to work and we haven't seen her since."

"Maybe she spent the night at a friend's place."

"Two nights ago," her mother said. "We haven't seen her for two nights. Do you think I would call if it was only one? She's never stayed away two nights in a row before."

And there was a time when she hadn't stayed out one, but lately it had been a regular occurrence. One night had certainly been nothing to write home about, and definitely nothing to warrant calling her ex-cop brother to look for her.

But two nights...

Alex stretched his neck and walked to the bed, pressing his hand against the imprint of where Nicole's body had been. Still warm from her body heat.

"Ma, I'm sure she's fine."

"But—"

"I'll check around for you if it will make you and Dad feel better."

"Oh, thank you, *agapemou*, thank you."

Alex punched the disconnect button then tossed the phone across the empty bed.

Athena was twenty-eight, no longer a child, and the only reason she still lived at home was because their parents wanted it that way. It was traditional in Greek culture that children lived at home until they married. And since Alex hadn't taken that route, it made Athena's situation doubly difficult. But while her mailing address might still be the Tudor-style house in Astoria, more and more often she stayed with one of her girlfriends in Manhattan, nearer to where she worked in Little Italy. The way he figured it, his parents should be happy she came home at all, considering the way they rode her. It was easy for him to avoid the "when are you getting married?", "when are you going to settle down?", "when are you going to get a real job?", "when are you going to continue the family name?" questions. He didn't have to see his parents nearly every day. Athena, on the other hand, described nightly dinner at the Cassavetes house as hell on earth.

So she up and disappeared for a day or two. The way he saw it, she was entitled. More than likely it was a survival technique. Much needed escape to keep herself from killing their overly protective, old-world parents.

He glared at the empty coffeepot, then pulled on his shoes and reached for his coat. Despite what he'd told his mother and despite his need for caffeine, the first challenge on his list was to find Nicole Bennett.

He turned toward the door, and nearly plowed right into her.

Alex stopped dead in his tracks. There she was, smelling of morning air and looking good enough to drink. He hadn't heard her come in, although the old door held no fewer than six locks. And he couldn't be sure how long she'd been there, given the way she leaned against a support post, a carrying case next to her feet. It could have been a minute; it could have been ten. Hell, she could have watched him since he was startled awake by his dream.

All he knew was that he'd never been more relieved to see anyone. And he feared that his objective to catch the thief wasn't the only motivation behind his reaction.

The sides of Nicole's mouth turned up in a naughty, knowing smile as she lifted an extralarge cup of coffee designed to satisfy anyone's caffeine cravings. "Thought you could use this."

Alex squinted at her. She was wearing a long, clingy black dress; what looked like combat boots that stretched to cover her knees, laced up the front, and had clunky heels; a shear black shirt that she had tied at the waist; and dozens of silver bracelets that clinked when she moved. He shook his head, wondering where she'd gotten the clothes but afraid to ask.

"So are you going to take it or what?" she asked.

"Mmm." Alex accepted the coffee, reasonably sure that she hadn't poisoned it since she'd gotten away and had come back on her own. He pulled the lid off and took a long pull of the hot liquid. "Where did you go?"

"To get a cuppa, of course." She glanced toward the kitchen. "That stuff you have isn't fit for a dog."

Fitting, seeing as he pretty much felt like a dog just then. An abused dog who didn't know where his next meal was coming from and whether or not the temptress in front of him would be the one to provide it.

He glanced at her wrists, then back at the bed. "How did you open the cuffs?"

Her smile widened. "Trade secret."

He nodded slowly. He'd concede that one. For now. But there was one question he wanted an answer to. And he wasn't at all convinced it was for strictly professional reasons.

He cleared his throat, keeping his gaze on her beautiful face. "Why did you come back?"

NOW THAT WAS A QUESTION.

Why had she come back?

Nicole slid her hands down her sides to rest firmly against her thighs, trying not to show her uneasiness.

The truth was, she wasn't clear on the reasons why she had returned to Alex's dark cavelike loft after leaving earlier that morning. She just knew that she had to. Because there was a rightness about his proposition that she couldn't blatantly ignore? Because he intrigued her unlike any other man had in a long, long time? Because he'd foiled her last job and would likely throw a monkey wrench into any other plans she put together until she agreed to work with him? Because condoms had prevented her from finding out if Alex would be as good at stroking her intimately as he was emotionally?

She eyed the way the red cotton of his T-shirt hugged his toned abdomen. "My intention had never been to leave."

He crossed his arms and stared at her, looking none too pleased with her disappearing and reappearing act. "I'm not following you here, Nicole."

She shrugged. "I merely wanted to prove a point."

"Ah." He leaned against the counter, looking way too sexy so early in the morning.

There were few guys who could pull off sexy before she'd had a full cup of coffee. Given her line of work, late nights were common, pushing back morning until almost noon. Rising before nine was like a death sentence to her, reducing her to little more than grumbles and glares until she fully woke up. Until then, humans resembled little more than intolerable trolls.

But just looking at Alex now made her want to climb back into that bed and put good use to the box of condoms she'd picked up along with the coffee.

"And that point would be?" Alex asked.

Nicole took the coffee from him and took a long sip before handing it back. "That I am where I am because I choose to be. Not because someone forced me to be."

She leaned over and unzipped the side of the carrying case. Her battle-scarred black cat bounded out, paused to look around, then set out to explore his new surroundings. Having spent the past few days in her friend Danika's cramped Village apartment, Cat appeared to approve of the change in scenery.

Nicole, however, was holding off judgment. She stepped farther into the two-story-high living area of the loft and took in the place in the light of day. Whoever had initially converted the space had done a piss-poor job of it. Cheap black paint covered everything in sight, from the wide beams crisscrossing overhead, to the cracked walls and the floor.

While black might be her favorite color, too much of a good thing was, well, too much. Besides, she half expected Dracula himself to step from the shadows at any moment and offer to add some color to the place. Namely red and by way of her blood.

"What's...that?"

"That's Cat. Cat, meet Alex. Alex, Cat."

The fearless feline crawled onto an old recliner, circled a few times, then plopped down right into the middle of it.

"I'm allergic."

"Nice try. Wherever I go, Cat goes."

A long pause.

"So you'll help me, then."

It was more a statement of fact than a question. Nicole slid a gaze over her shoulder. "You need to fire your interior decorator."

He grimaced at her nonanswer. "That would be my mother. Or at least it would be if I let her at the place."

Nicole gestured with her hand. "Anything has to be better than this."

"Oh?" he asked. "I would have thought the color scheme would be right up your alley." His gaze traveled slowly down her body, then back up again, sending shivers scooting everywhere. "And, trust me. What my mother has in mind would be worse. Think green tassels and gold Greek Orthodox icons covering the entire wall."

Nicole shuddered, but she wasn't altogether sure it was a result of the picture he painted.

Silence reigned as she turned back and pretended to study the apartment.

She had to give Alex credit. Despite apprehending her in Baltimore, then cuffing her to his bed, he didn't rush things. He asked a question, then gave her the space she needed to answer it.

Finally, she said, "Let's say we'll help each other."

Alex put the coffee down on the counter, then came to stand next to her. The stairs to the upper part of the loft were to their left. A black wrought-iron railing followed them up then ran the length of what looked like a good-sized second floor with a view of the lower floor. "And what, exactly, do you plan to get out of all of this?" he asked quietly. "I mean, aside from a temporary 'keep out of jail' card?"

Nicole notched her chin up. "I get to help nail the man who put my father behind bars."

SHE WAS ON BOARD.

Two hours later, Alex's triumph had faded, leaving him unsure if he was still happy about the arrangement. Because Nicole seemed bound and determined to make good on her comment about working together. He'd gone over everything he had so far, filled her in on some of the background information, and basically ground his teeth when she interrupted every five seconds with questions. The main problem being that those questions made him concentrate on her and her sexy mouth instead of the hunt.

This wasn't exactly the way he saw this...collaboration working out. Just when he thought he had everything figured out, Nicole would launch another one of her scud missiles in his direction and render him speechless. Not that it was difficult. Unfortunately just looking at her struck him dumb.

Of course, his idea had been to keep her handcuffed to his bed. Which, in his opinion, was still a pretty good idea. If only to give him enough time to go buy some friggin' condoms.

He quickened his step to keep up with her as she led the way down Houston Street, resisting the urge to drop a couple of steps behind her so he might watch her walk. Okay. So there was something about a woman wearing a snug black cotton skirt that brought out the ogler in any guy. The way the material slipped and hugged her delectably shaped bottom and thighs as she moved drove him insane. And the contrast of the military-style shiny leather boots only made her that much more enticing.

A strange enigma, this Black Cat Nicole Bennett. Oh,

she may have told him that her father was doing a nickel in prison, but she hadn't offered much else aside from Dark Man having been involved in the crime. And whatever Nicole knew...well, she wasn't sharing. After all, she'd pointed out, that wasn't important, was it? What was important was that they got this guy.

What was important to him... Well, maybe important wasn't the word. He tugged at the collar of his T-shirt. What was more of a curiosity, really, was to discover that under Nicole's tough-as-nails exterior, she was human. She had a family she cared about.

"We should go to my office," he said, surprised to find that they were only a block away from the building the insurance offices were located in. "Go through the material I've compiled there. See if there's something you can pick up on that I've missed."

Nicole stared at him, a stubborn look on her face, but didn't say anything.

He grimaced. Definitely not the way he saw this going down.

Okay, whatever point she might be trying to make, he'd give her the room to make it. Because the simple truth was he needed her to make this collar. To unmask the infamous Dark Man. He'd hit a wall months ago in his investigation, even as new crimes were committed and the theft-related death toll rose. That he'd as good as kidnapped Nicole Bennett was a clear enough sign that he was open to taking desperate measures. Allowing her to call the shots this morning...well, it wouldn't be any more unusual than anything he'd already done in the past couple of days.

Nicole's step slowed and she opened the door to a coffee shop he knew well. It was within walking distance of the insurance company and served moder-

ately good coffee along with muffins, donuts, burgers
and a small menu of short-order stuff. He'd been there
a time or two, but preferred the cleaner environment of
the restaurant up the street. She led the way toward a
free booth in the middle of the long, narrow establishment and scooted in, her back to the door.

Odd. He would have thought she'd sit with her eye
on everything going on. He started to sit on the other
side of the table when she grasped his wrist and indicated he should scoot in next to her.

He didn't get it, but his body was in full agreement
with the suggestion. Nicole leaned toward him. "Don't
worry, I don't bite." She smiled and the very devil
seemed to dance in her dark eyes. "Unless you want
me to, that is."

His libido immediately let him know it was in favor
of whatever she had in mind.

A female voice behind him was saying, "Work,
work, work. I swear, they should have five people to
do the job I'm doing. Or at least pay me a damn sight
better than they are."

Nicole held up two fingers toward the waitress and
within seconds their coffee cups were filled.

"Anything else?" the waitress asked.

Nicole looked at him.

Alex realized she was waiting for a response. "Um,
no. Nothing more for me, thanks."

"Fine." The waitress moved on to the next table.

"I don't get it," Alex said.

Nicole lightly tapped her finger against her lips, indicating he should be quiet.

Great. Just great. He needed questions answered,

had a big-time crook to catch, and she didn't feel like talking.

Nicole smiled that sexy little knowing smile and silently sipped her black coffee.

The woman's voice behind him continued, "Take this morning, for example. My boss slaps a folder as thick as a Danielle Steele novel on my desk and tells me he needs the policy put together stat. Stat," she snorted. "Like what we do is a matter of life or death or something."

Policy? Alex moved to turn his head, but Nicole stayed him with a hand on his arm. He stared at her. She discreetly nodded toward a large grimy mirror in the back of the establishment that was tilted to reflect everything and everyone in the diner.

Alex heard a quiet response to the woman's complaint behind him from her companion, another female.

"And you wouldn't believe what this policy is for. I swear, give a guy some money and turn him stupid."

Alex couldn't see anything more than the back of the speaker's blond head in the mirror, but watched as she waved her hand.

"I mean, whoever heard of insuring a cockatiel for a quarter of a million dollars? A friggin' cockatiel."

She sighed. "Anyway, I shouldn't be telling you all this, you know, being against company policy and all. But I guess it's not too bad, seeing as you work there, too. Anyway, who else would believe it?"

Alex's gaze moved beyond the speaker to the woman she was talking to and nearly choked on the coffee he was taking a sip of. It was the policy clerk in the office down the hall from his.

"Anyway, we really should be getting back to work," the speaker was saying. "Seeing as we have all those important idiots to protect and all."

Alex sat dumbfounded as the two women left the booth, gathered their purses and doggie bags, then left the coffee shop.

"You can move to the other side now," Nicole said, keeping her gaze on her coffee cup as she took a long sip.

Alex's gaze followed the move, zooming in on her full, luscious lips. She drank like she lived: dangerously. She didn't seem to care that the coffee was hot or that there was someone watching her. The way she fastened those maddening lips on the rim made him think of certain areas of his anatomy that would be happy for the attention.

It took him a full minute and her raised brow for him to finally register what she'd said.

He moved to the other side of the booth.

"You know what your problem is?" Nicole said.

Oh, he had a pretty good idea. He was attracted to her, that's what his problem was. No, not attracted. Attracted was too tame a word for what he felt for the bad girl across from him. He'd been blindsided by her. Was obsessed with the thought of easing between her thighs and finding out if she felt as good as she tasted.

He had no doubt she did.

Nicole's half smile told him she probably knew where his mind was. "You think too much like a cop."

Alex blinked. "And that's a problem how?" He leaned forward to get the sugar and cream from the end of the table. "You know, seeing as my background in law enforcement got me my job."

She absently ran her fingertip around the rim of her cup. Alex noted her black-painted short nails and the softness of her hands. "You have no finesse."

Alex didn't think that was a compliment, but he thanked her just the same.

She laughed quietly. "What I'm saying is that you're used to barging into a situation, asking questions and expecting to get answers when sometimes just shutting up and listening is the best course of action."

Alex squinted toward the door the two company employees had just exited. "How many jobs you pick up on from those two?"

Nicole shrugged. "One or two."

"I'll have them fired."

Her smile widened. "There you go. Barging in again."

"And what would you have me do?"

"First I would have you ask yourself if you really think they are the only two individuals innocently discussing company business during their personal lunch hour." She shrugged. "Fire them and the two who take their place will be exactly the same. They're underpaid, overworked and to make it through the day they have to vent. You should be thankful they're doing it with each other instead of outsiders."

Alex frowned. "I'll talk to the higher-ups. Get them to make employees take lunch on the premises."

She laughed. A rich, genuine sound that caught Alex off guard. "Has anyone ever told you that you're funny?"

"No." He drank his coffee, thinking funny was the last thing he wanted to be to her in that moment. "So is there any other reason we need to be here?"

Her gaze caught on the mirror and her smile slipped. Alex glanced to see a young, nice-looking man entering the eatery.

"I'll be back in a minute," she said as the man passed by their table.

WHAT WAS HER BROTHER Jeremy doing here?

Nicole pushed from the bench seat and straightened her skirt, acutely aware of Alex's gaze on her, wreaking havoc on her senses. When he looked at her, there was something...different somehow in his eyes. Physical need, yes. But there also lurked a hunger that nearly singed her with merely a glance. A craving that ignited an answering one in her, cutting the bottom out of her stomach and robbing the bone from her knees.

The combination of that indecipherable desire, and the confusion of seeing her brother in the last place he should be, made her dizzy.

It probably didn't help that she'd put nothing in her mouth but coffee since lunch yesterday, but she wasn't going to think about that right now.

"Imagine running into you here," she said when Jeremy took a stool at the counter near the back of the diner.

"Nic!"

Younger than her by two years, Jeremy towered over her by at least a foot, and was light where she was dark. She looked into his familiar blue eyes and took in his handsomely tousled blond hair...and suppressed the urge to cuff him one.

"What? Why are you looking at me like that?" he said after he hugged her.

"You know why," she whispered harshly, taking the stool next to him. "How are Joanna and Justine?"

Namely, his wife of the past year and infant daughter. The two women who had supposedly changed his life forever.

"They're fine." Jeremy gave her a wide, unabashed grin. "Justine's sleeping on her own now. No more midnight feedings."

"So does that mean you can go out on some midnight creepings?"

Jeremy's smile slipped. "Oh, Nic, come on. You know I'm out of the business. I haven't pulled any jobs in over twelve months."

She caught the way he scratched his right palm. "Then what are you doing here?"

"You know, other people's sisters would ask, 'Bro, how the hell are you doing? What brings you out to this neck of the cement woods? Buy you a cup?'" His grin made a return. "But not you. No. Instead you automatically assume I'm pulling jobs again." The waitress behind the counter filled his coffee cup and he ordered a breakfast plate. "Nope, the only thing I'm working on is other people's plumbing." He waggled his brows at her. "And on Joanna's, of course."

Nicole relaxed, but only a little.

Jeremy loved his wife and infant daughter. She knew that as sure as she knew that what she'd be wearing tomorrow would be black. But she also knew that there were only a handful of places in Manhattan where a working thief could go to pick up on reliable secondhand information, and Coffee Corner was one of them. Seeing as it wasn't a place one went out of their way to have a meal at, Jeremy's presence was suspicious at best.

He smiled at her. "If you want to know the truth, I'm down here to talk to Demasi about a job. You know, something part-time to help bridge the gaps."

"Bruno?" And he was telling her he was out of the business? Bruno Demasi was one of the biggest thieves this side of the Hudson.

"Ah. I thought you might not have heard."

"Heard what?" She was an inch away from hauling him back to the john and giving him a swirly until he swore he wouldn't put his future with his new family at risk.

His grin was almost smug. "That he started his own security firm. You know, instead of taking, he now protects the stuff he would have taken." He shrugged. "I hear he's doing pretty good and the word's out that he's taking on new personnel. Hell, if I had something to protect, he'd be the first person I'd hire."

"Bruno, a security guard? That big lug?"

Jeremy chuckled. "I'd like to see you say that to his face."

Of course she never would, not if she hoped to keep her own face. Bruno was a hothead. He was also one of the best thieves running today.

"Dad asked about you last Sunday," Jeremy said quietly.

The air rushed from Nicole's lungs, all thought of Big Bruno and his new gig vanishing from her mind.

Those were the absolute last words she expected to hear come out of her brother's mouth. Some comment on the weather, maybe. An aside about how he'd heard so-and-so had done such-and-such. But never anything concerning their father.

Jeremy scanned her face. "Yeah, Joanna and I took the baby up to visit him." He drank out of his water glass. "He says you haven't been out since he got locked up."

Nicole stared straight ahead, feeling the blood rush from her face.

"Any particular reason why you haven't been out?"

"I've been busy."

"So have I, but I don't let that stop me."

She started to get up. "Let it go, Jer. At least you and your family are going up. That's enough for now."

She made the mistake of looking at him. At seeing the curious shadow in his eyes. "He wants to see you."

And she wanted to see him. So badly it hurt. But she couldn't do it while he was in there. Couldn't bear to see him behind bars. Even if the address of his current residence didn't bother him in the least, just knowing what all that cement and metal represented—namely, the loss of freedom—made her queasy.

Nicole quickly kissed her brother on the cheek. "Give Joanna and Justine my love, you hear? Maybe I'll stop by sometime this week."

"I'd rather you stopped by to see Dad."

Nicole ignored his comment as she passed Alex and told him they were leaving.

5

WHO WAS THAT GUY back at the coffee shop and what in the hell did he want from Nicole?

Alex stood in the elevator next to the tight-lipped woman in question, none too happy about the attention she garnered from the men packed in the elevator with them. The attention she garnered from everyone wherever she went.

He rubbed the back of his neck, irritated in a way that he'd never been before.

He was jealous.

It was as simple and as complicated as that.

He let rip a series of silent curse words. Never, ever, in his thirty-two-year existence could he remember being jealous. So unfamiliar was he with the emotion that he hadn't nailed it for what it was straight off. He'd thought at the root of his irritation lay pure, unadulterated sexual frustration, and his prolonged need to put his quarry behind bars. Instead, the fact that other men wanted Nicole Bennett as much as he did made him want to punch a few lights out.

Definitely a new experience for him. And not one he was particularly comfortable with. He'd never challenged the grade-school bully to a fight and couldn't imagine starting now.

"Afternoon, Alex."

He glanced over at Jason Dewitt, one of the dweebs

from accounting, then followed the man's gaze to Nicole's breasts. "Jason," he ground out. Then he nodded at John Carlon who worked down the hall from him. "John."

John lowered his voice and lightly elbowed Alex as he stared at Nicole's cleavage as well. "New client?"

Alex grimaced at his co-worker. Only John was more than that, so he couldn't fault him for his actions. He had been the one to show Alex the ropes when he first hired on at the company, and he'd offered him the type of camaraderie he'd experienced on the force. If he had any questions or needed any backup, John was the first one he went to. He was also the first one to want to grab a beer after an especially hard day of tedious business meetings.

Unfortunately, he was leaving the company, having accepted a prime position with a rival firm in San Francisco. Alex smiled at his friend. "So, John, I hear Friday is your last day here."

"Yeah. We'll have to grab a beer or something before I go." John looked at Nicole again. "How's tonight?"

"Sorry, buddy, no can do. But let's definitely arrange something."

The elevator dinged when it reached the twenty-fifth floor and he and John set up tentative plans. Then the doors opened and Nicole and her sexy boots led the way out, earning stares as she passed the desks situated around the large open area between the closed offices.

"Excuse me," one of the secretaries said as she stood in the middle of the pathway, her arms loaded with folders so that Nicole had no choice but to bump into her as she passed.

"You're excused," Nicole said.

Alex coughed behind his hand. She glanced at him, a mischievous gleam in her dark eyes as if she was well aware of the effect she had on people and that she enjoyed using it to her advantage.

He crossed in front of her and opened his office door, motioning for her to precede him in. He took the unguarded moment to appreciate what his co-workers had.

Nicole Bennett was va-va-vavoom in capital letters.

And he wanted to cover her up. Put a bag over her head and a potato sack over those luscious curves.

The problem was she'd still look good enough to eat.

He watched as she stopped in the middle of the room and looked around. He noticed the way her shoulders went stiff and knew exactly what she was looking at.

He stepped inside and closed the door on at least five associates craning their necks straining to get a look inside.

At a little over fifteen by fifteen, the only saving grace for his office was its large window overlooking the edge of the financial district...and the fact that the display board next to the door was filled with photos of the very woman looking at it now.

"Jesus," she murmured, moving from shot to shot.

Alex released the lock, then tapped the bottom of the revolving board until the white dry-erase side was facing them. Then he pushed the entire display back against the wall. He rounded his desk and unlocked the drawer with the file on Dark Man inside. He took it out and laid it on the cluttered desktop.

He heard Nicole swallow. "Did you, um, take all those?"

He didn't have to ask what she was referring to. It was obvious the pictures of her had made an impact. "No. I subcontract a local P.I. to work on cases like yours. A woman by the name of Kylie Capshaw took most of those."

She slowly turned to face him, her eyes wary and watchful. "Don't you have any other cases?"

He gestured to the pile of twenty or so case files in his in-box.

Nicole idly fingered through them, but he could tell she wasn't seeing them. Instead, her mind was apparently on the board and the pictures of her now facing the wall. Alex squinted, trying to read her expression. He realized she looked...vulnerable somehow. Exposed.

And he suddenly hated that he was the one who had made her feel that way.

"You're not the target, Nic," he murmured.

Her gaze snapped to his face, seeming surprised at his use of the shortened name.

"Is it okay if I call you that?"

She shrugged as if it was of no consequence to her, although he suspected it was.

"This it?" she asked, turning the file he had just opened so she could look through it.

"Yes."

She sat on the edge of the desk and began quickly leafing through what had taken him months to compile. He picked up the phone and asked his secretary Dorothy to bring in all the policies that had been issued over the past couple of months for over a hundred thousand.

"Make it a half," Nicole said.

He changed the amount then hung up the extension.

She tapped a page in front of her. "He's upping the ante. Each job bigger than the one before."

Alex didn't need to point out that the rate of casualties had also risen as he sat on the other side of the desk and noticed her fingering a blurry picture. "We think that might be him."

She picked up the snapshot of the shadowy figure and held it out to stare at it. She didn't say anything as she put it back down.

"Did your father get a good look at him while they were working together?"

Nicole's movements slowed. "I didn't say they worked together."

"Sorry. My mistake. When you said he was responsible for your father's imprisonment, I assumed..."

"Natural assumption." She crossed her arms. "Cramped office."

He looked around and smiled. "A bit."

"I'd go crazy in a place like this inside a week."

Alex had no doubt that she would. "I thought the same thing when I first hired on." He shrugged. "But you get used to it. Learn to distract yourself."

"With things like looking for D.M."

Dark Man.

"Something like that."

She took a deep breath. "My father never saw him." She looked directly at Alex. "No one has. At least no one I know about."

He considered her. "You've been asking around."

It wasn't a question and she didn't answer. Instead she glanced toward the closed door, then back at him. "Do you have access to all the policies underwritten?"

"High-end luxury items, yes."

She nodded.

"Why?"

"Because the sweaty short guy who was staring at my breasts in the elevator sells information on such policies to the highest bidder."

"Dewitt?" Alex nearly fell off the side of his desk. "He works in accounting."

"Mmm. Guess he wanted in on some of the numbers he crunches. You might want to do some cross-checking. I bet the policies he can get his hands on easily coincide with a high percentage of thefts. He could be more original and look for more difficult policies, but he strikes me as the lazy type."

Alex looked at her. Really looked at her. Sure she was sexy as all get out. And even now he wanted to haul her across his desk and have another go at her. But she was also incredibly smart. And she didn't offer up information as a braggart might, but rather as a statement of fact.

He also found it curious that while she didn't come out and say how she felt about someone like Dewitt doing what he did, there was an undercurrent of disapproval in her voice.

He found his gaze skimming her figure and cleared his throat. "How much does information like that go for?"

Her pupils seemed to grow huge in her eyes as she watched him. "Depends on the score."

"A percentage?"

"No," she said, shaking her head and causing that black silky hair to stir then settle back into place. "Too risky. A pat amount. One hundred. Two hundred. A grand."

"That's quite a scale."

"Mmm. Like I said, it depends on the score."

He wished she'd stop using that word. Every time she said "score" he thought of "scoring" with her.

He pretended interest in putting the file back together. "Have you ever bought info from him?"

"No. But I know those who have." He heard the smile in her voice, as if she sensed what he was thinking and was slightly amused by it.

She also appeared slightly turned on as she recrossed her legs and scooted a little closer to him on the desk. The spicy scent of her skin teased his nose and the close proximity of her breasts made it all but impossible to think.

Alex resisted the urge to tug on the collar of his T-shirt. "Ah. Would these be the same people you target?"

She laughed. "No. These would be friends."

"And you don't steal from friends."

"No, I don't steal from friends."

Silence stretched between them. A sensually charged silence that seemed to notch up the temperature in the small office and make Alex's T-shirt feel like a woolen parka.

"I thought honor among thieves extended to all thieves," he said, wondering if she'd really moved closer or whether wishful thinking was what made her now seem close enough to kiss.

"Nope." Was it him, or was her voice huskier than

before? "Thieves are like the rest of the professional population. And those who act without honor don't deserve to be honored."

During the conversation, Alex paid close attention to the slight change in her body language. Where she'd grown tense at the sight of her pictures on the board, she now seemed to relax, leaning back against her arms, her long silky black hair slanting over her shoulder and down over her breasts. He was finding it increasingly difficult not to look at those sweet mounds of flesh beneath the stretchy, low-cut fabric of her dress. So he stopped trying to fight it.

What did that make him given their current surroundings? Not any better than Dewitt. He lifted his gaze to Nicole's face to find her eyes sparkling suggestively at him. Then again, maybe there was a whole world of difference.

"You should turn your desk to face the window. A shame to waste such a great view."

Speaking of great views...

"What's stopping you?"

Alex blinked. "Excuse me?"

Nicole shrugged, causing the sheer blouse she wore to dip down over one pale shoulder. He discovered the dress she had on underneath didn't have sleeves and that under that she didn't have on a bra as she dipped a finger under one strap and eased it down over her arm until the material stretched across her left breast.

"What's stopping you from acting on what you so obviously want to do?" she murmured.

A click sounded as Alex swallowed. Oh, about five hundred of his co-workers on the other side of the door, for one thing.

He cleared his throat. "And what is it that you, um, think I want to do?"

"Mmm. Touch me, maybe?"

Oh, yeah. That and a whole lot more. "Because I don't think it would be a very good idea." He put the file back in his desk drawer.

She allowed her gaze to travel the length of him and back again and he felt his arousal grow. "Why not?"

"A dozen different reasons," he said, increasingly unable to come up with a single one.

She chuckled quietly, sexily. "You know what your problem is, Alex?"

"I think too much like a cop."

She didn't respond for a long moment. "You operate by too many rules."

He cracked a smile. "And you operate by too few. I guess in the end it balances things out, doesn't it?"

"Maybe." She lowered her lashes, considering her own breasts and the way she was using them to tantalize him. "And maybe you need to crawl over onto this end of the teeter-totter. Find out how much fun it is on this side."

Alex's body temperature had risen so high he swore his neck burned. Last night in the Theisman family guest room he'd gotten but a taste. And fun wasn't the word he'd use to describe what having sex with Nicole would be like. Outstanding, phenomenal, sinful were words that came to mind.

But despite how much he wanted her, he knew he shouldn't allow himself to have her. She was a thief. And she was now officially a co-worker.

And, frankly, the thought that sex with her would

far surpass even his imagination scared the crap out of him.

Still, before he knew what he was doing, he'd reached out and tugged that strap a little farther down her arm until her nipple slipped out of the front.

His breath caught in his throat. While he'd laved that same breast the night before, everything had been done in the dark where things that might not happen otherwise regularly took place. But here in his office in the middle of the day with the afternoon sunlight slanting through the window behind him, there were no such excuses, no shadows to hide behind, no darkness to blame.

Her areola covered nearly the entire circumference of her breast, large and a deep burgundy color. His mouth watered with the craving to feel her skin against his tongue again. She shifted, forcing the material down even farther, her breathing shallow, her tongue dipping out to moisten her full, provocative lips.

"So are you going to kiss me or what?"

Alex blinked until he was looking into the intoxicating depths of her eyes.

Good God, but he was afraid that if anyone could tempt him to cross the line of the law, it would be this dark temptress.

NICOLE'S HEART beat a slow, uneven rhythm beneath her breastbone, making it impossible to draw in the air that she needed. The cool air from an overhead vent spilled over her bare skin, further puckering her nipple and making her shiver even as pure, scorching heat rushed to her lower abdomen.

She wanted this man between her legs. *Now.* She

didn't care that at any moment his secretary would be coming through that door. That on the other side of that board were pictures of her that she hadn't known had been taken. That she was pretty sure the occupants in the building across the street could see what they were doing through the windows.

"Or what," Alex rasped, finally answering her question then leaning over to run his tongue along her swollen nipple.

Nicole gasped, the blatant show of desire the last thing she expected from him. Her back automatically arched and she grasped the edge of the desk to keep from toppling off the side. Ripples of sheer pleasure rushed over her skin, leaving her breathless and hot, so very hot.

Alex's actions ceased and Nicole blinked open her eyelids to find him looking at her. She hadn't realized she'd closed her eyes until then. He groaned then tugged on her knees, pulling her until her legs dangled over his side of the desk, mindless of the files that plunged to the floor as he edged his way between her thighs and pressed himself against the crotch of her panties.

Nicole grasped his shoulders to catch her balance, then scooted until her bottom was at the very edge of the desk making for a fuller meeting between his body and hers.

Then he finally kissed her.

For a blissful instant Nicole forgot entirely where she was. Red-hot sensation poured over her, through her, as his tongue tangled with hers, claiming her mouth in a way that was ravenous yet gentle, demanding yet pleading, so unlike the awkward kiss from the night before. This was a man who was sure of what he wanted, was even surer that he shouldn't want it, and was going ahead and taking it anyway.

Nicole lifted her hands to his face and pulled him closer yet, her palms rasping over the slight stubble on his jaw. She moved her head right to left then back again, wanting to swallow him whole.

She felt Alex's hands on her knees, lingering at the top of her boots, then seeking out the flesh just above them.

Slow, too slow, Nicole thought for the second time in as many days. She reached down and hiked up the cotton of her skirt then placed his hand directly between her legs.

A shudder so profound she was afraid she might climax wracked her body. She caught herself with her hands on the desk behind her, then jerked her hips upward, sliding her swollen womanhood against the thick ridge bulging beneath his jeans.

Nice. Very nice, indeed.

He bent to lick her exposed breast and she watched him, captivated by the darkening of his green eyes, the pained pleasure on his face. He pressed his palm against her chest, slowly forcing her to lie flat against the desk. Nicole's breath caught in her throat as she watched him slide that same hand down the middle of her abdomen, lower and lower until the heel of his palm ground against the pulse point between her legs. She gasped. But when she thought the sensation couldn't be any stronger without penetration, he worked his index finger under the elastic of her panties and drew his knuckle over the engorged flesh then down through her narrow, wet channel.

There was a knock at the door. Nicole heard another gasp, and realized it hadn't come from either her or Alex.

"I'm sorry. I'll, um, come back later."

The closing of the door.

· Nicole would have laughed at the secretary's reaction, if she hadn't been so damn hot she thought she might spontaneously combust.

She reached to keep Alex centered, but he was already gone, having removed his hand and stepped away, staring at her as if just realizing she was in the room.

She pushed up onto her elbows. "Don't tell me that's the first time you've done something like this in here."

His voice sounded grave. "Okay, I won't."

Reluctantly she raised to a sitting position and swung her legs back and forth in an effort to burn up unused energy that, unfortunately, she didn't think was going to be used anytime soon. Not with Alex looking like he was considering jumping out the window.

She pushed from the desk and repositioned certain areas of her dress.

Alex's gaze followed her movements. "I'll just go get those files."

WHAT WAS HE THINKING?

Or, more accurately, what part of his body had he been thinking with?

He'd left his office to collect the files from the shell-shocked secretary he shared with four other investigators, but ended up passing her desk in favor of the men's room and lots of cold running water. He scooped it up and over his face again and again until his skin was numb.

He stared at his dripping face in the mirror and reached for a wad of paper towels. Had he really been about to have sex with Nicole right there on his desk?

He grew rock-hard just thinking about it, answering his own questions.

Oh, yes, he wanted her. But on his terms. And what had happened in the other room had been on her terms. Nicole appeared to be into sexual power games. She was a woman who could never be happy with just plain sex in a bed with sheets and an alarm clock on the bedside table. She craved excitement, spontaneity and out-of-your-mind passion.

And he'd been just a hairbreadth away from giving it to her.

He mopped the water from his face, thrust his fingers through his tousled hair, then stalked back toward his office.

"Do you have the files, Dorothy?"

The secretary blinked at him. "Your...she...the woman you were, um, meeting with took them."

Alex pushed open his office door to find Nicole sitting in his desk chair going through the files in question. He crossed the room and took them out of her hands. "That's classified information."

"Not anymore."

He glanced at her over the top of the first file. "How did you get them from Dorothy, anyway?"

"Isn't it funny how some women react to seeing another woman's bare breasts?" She shook her head. "I could have asked her for the key to the company safe and she probably would have given it to me."

Alex grimaced as he walked across the room.

"He'll target the client in the file I put on top," Nicole said, getting up from his desk.

He scanned the term policy taken out by a high-end auction house set to sell off an impressive estate art collection next Tuesday. Interesting, but...

"Actually something just occurred to me." He squinted at her. "What if we were to fabricate a policy? I have a wealthy client who's in Europe for the next few weeks so I know his house is empty. We could make up a story saying he bought, I don't know, say, some of those Double Eagle coins that are making the news lately and is taking out a policy to cover them."

"What are Double Eagles?"

"They're uncirculated 1933 twenty-dollar gold pieces. There are only a few known to be in existence and they're nabbing a king's ransom at last check." He tapped a pen against the folder she'd pointed out. "We could issue this fake policy then make sure it was leaked. Then all we would have to do is case the empty house and wait for D.M. to go after the literal loot."

"He's too thorough for that. He'd smell a setup a mile away."

He watched her pick up her backpack and walk past him toward the door. "Where are you going?"

She stopped just inside and leaned against the wooden barrier. "You always ask this many questions?"

He did when so much of his life and career hung in the balance.

"I'll see you later."

Alex stared at the empty air she'd left in her wake and frowned.

See him later, when? At his apartment? Here?

He rounded his desk and sank into his chair. The woman was trouble with a capital *T*. He opened his desk drawer to take out the D.M. file. Only when he reached in, his hand closed around something else instead. More specifically, a square clear plastic packet through the side of which he could see a bright purple condom.

He opened the other four drawers finding different colored prophylactics in all of them.

Holy Mother of God.

He gathered them up and slid them into his pocket, only to find another one in there.

He grinned. He had to admit, she had style.

6

THE OLD WINDUP CLOCK ticked the seconds away on the bedside table. Alex picked it up and stared at the face in the dim light from the quarter moon hanging outside his multipaned windows. After 2:00 a.m. and he hadn't been able to close his eyes yet. After 2:00 a.m. and even Manhattan was quiet, the occasional police siren and odd car going by on the streets outside. After 2:00 a.m. and he hadn't heard from Nicole since 2:00 p.m., when she'd walked out of his office with the promise that she'd see him later.

The old bedsprings squeaked as he put the clock back down, then shifted into a more comfortable position on his back. The problem was that in two minutes he'd have to shift again because no position was comfortable for long. Not because he wasn't physically tired. Rather his mind roared ahead at sixty miles per hour, going over the things he had said and done with Nicole. And driving him insane with the possibilities of what she might be doing at that exact moment.

He glanced toward the window to the far left. The one that Nicole had opened just enough to let her damn cat out. He hadn't spotted the furball so he assumed he was outside somewhere terrorizing the neighborhood, even though the food bowl she'd put out in the kitchen proved he'd been in to eat. Which was just fine with him. Nicole was enough to contend with. He didn't have it in him to contend with her cat, too.

Over his past four-month investigation of her, she'd had no fewer than three boyfriends. If the term "boyfriend" could even apply to a man Nicole went out with. Lover seemed closer, but even that implied a longtime commitment. From what he could tell, she didn't know the definition of the word commitment. She met a guy—the first at a dance club, the second at a coffee shop, the third at an after-show party of an off-off-Broadway play—she dated him briefly, then she moved on like a restless raven looking for a better view on another tree.

He rubbed his face with his hands then stretched his arms up over his head, closing his eyes. The thing was, while he knew a lot of superficial information, he knew absolutely zip when it came to the emotional foundation of the very sexy, very cunning Nicole Bennett. She'd mentioned a father. Was there a mother in the picture? What about siblings? How did she feel about the world at large, and family life in particular? Did a house in the suburbs appeal to her, or would she rather live in perpetual motion in the city, moving from man to man, flophouse to flophouse?

Simply, she was the wildest, most eccentric person he'd ever met. Not above sharing a couple of her trade secrets with him by way of demonstration rather than telling. And not hesitant about telling him how she felt about him. Which was pretty much how he felt about her. Namely, he wanted to have sex with her so bad the mere thought of the possibility gave him a rock-hard erection.

He'd had two relationships in his life. Serious ones.

Then again, those were the only ones he'd had. While he'd sowed his oats a bit at NYU by sleeping with a couple of fellow students, casual sex had never been his thing. No. There was all that postcoital awkwardness. Rather, Jenny Callas had been his first girlfriend, from age seventeen until well into his sophomore year in college. Why had that ended? He rubbed the line of his brow with his thumb. Oh, that's right. Jenny had broken it off when he hadn't shown an interest in getting married and starting a family while he was still at university.

A year or two after that he'd entered into a semi-arranged relationship with Natassa Hurley, whose Greek mother had met his mother through the church. Natassa worked at her mother's bakery, was pretty and turned out to be pretty good company. But eventually she, too, had started talking marriage, about his coming into the bakery with her, and he refused to participate in the conversation. Now, a year later, she was married to a Polish guy and had a baby and as far as he could tell, she led a happy life living in the apartment above the bakery.

Marriage. His mother sometimes asked if he had something against it, if there was something he'd seen in his parents' marriage to scare him away from it. He'd answered her honestly. That no, he had nothing against it. But it hadn't felt right with Jenny or Natassa. While he'd cared for both women, when he'd looked into their eyes he hadn't seen beyond that moment. No tomorrow. No children lurking in there begging to be let out. Nothing solid or concrete on which to build a relationship that was intended to last for life.

He sighed.

And Nicole?

Hell, if there was a model to be used for what not to look for in a wife, it was her.

He grimaced, imagining how his parents would react to her.

But his parents' approval wasn't all that made her bad marriage material. There was the little detail that she lived on the wrong side of the law. Darted in and out of the shadows that inevitably would one day not hide her well enough and she would be left facing serious punishment for her crimes. Her father was in prison, for Christ's sake. How did you explain that one to your children? "Of course you have a grandpa, son, but he's indisposed at the moment because he did something very bad."

What was he thinking? Nicole scrambled his gray matter in a way that didn't allow him to think, period. For that reason alone he could never imagine more than a hot tryst with her. He couldn't see them twenty years down the road, him wondering where she was, whose jewelry she was pilfering and wanting her so much that he didn't care about either.

But he did want her. So badly it hurt.

The sound of metal teeth ratcheting then the feel of cold metal encircling his wrist where he had his arm stretched above his head let him know he was no longer alone.

"Mmm. Penny for your thoughts," Nicole whispered against his ear. Her hair teased the skin on his shoulder as she tested the soundness of the handcuffs she'd just fastened around his wrist.

Alex didn't open his eyes immediately. Instead he breathed in the spicy scent of her.

She'd come back.

In that one moment, it didn't matter where she had been, or what kind of trouble she might have gotten into, or even whether or not she had broken the law. What emerged as important to him just then was that they use every last one of the condoms she'd left behind in his office.

He felt fingertips walk over his erection through his snug cotton boxers and groaned.

"Did you miss me?" she whispered, gripping him in her hand. "I think you did."

How could he miss what he hadn't had yet? Instead, he was driving himself crazy thinking about getting it.

Alex heard the sound of material rasping against skin and cracked his eyelids open to find her stripping from the boots, blouse and dress she'd had on earlier. The moonlight kissed her pale skin and turned her dark hair into a black cloud, making her look almost ethereal. Which was definitely not a word he'd generally use to describe Nicole Bennett. Sinfully sexy, unabashedly bold, uninhibitedly decadent, but never ethereal.

He swallowed as he realized he'd been right about her not wearing a bra earlier. Her breasts were well shaped, not too large, not too small, and were pert and full, in perfect proportion to the rest of her body.

Then there was that underwear…

Alex tried to reach for her, only to find that she'd handcuffed his right hand to the headboard. Using his left would be awkward at best, and make him look desperate at worst.

She flashed him a knowing smile as she drew a finger around and around his right nipple, then tweaked the bit of flesh. "I figure after last night, turnabout is fair play."

Alex wanted to open his mouth to object, to remind her that he hadn't abused the opportunity provided by her being handcuffed to his bed. But the truth was there was something dangerously exciting about being shackled to his own bed, unable to move. He'd been a cop for eight years and had heard his co-workers talk about the ways they'd used cuffs that you wouldn't find in any procedural manual, but it had never occurred to him to use them himself outside of what was dictated by his job.

He watched as Nicole climbed on top of the bed then straddled him, her hot bottom resting against the tops of his legs. Good God, she was going to end him right there and then. She gathered her hair over on one side of her head then leaned forward to tantalizingly brush her lips against his.

"Mmm...I've been thinking about this all day," she murmured, dipping her tongue between his lips and taking inventory before darting back out again.

He cleared his throat, thinking he should say something that didn't make him sound like a lustful moron. "And what did that day entail, exactly?"

She pulled back a bit and smiled down at him. "There was this really hot, really uptight guy that I spent a good part of the time with."

He didn't have to ask if she was talking about him. Uptight was his middle name.

"And I've come to a conclusion about him."

Alex swallowed the saliva collecting at the back of his mouth. "Oh?"

"Mmm-hmm." She sucked on her index finger then

played with his nipple again. "I've decided that this guy, you know, that I met? Well, he needs to learn how to loosen up a bit. Cut loose. Act on his impulses instead of analyze them."

She slipped her finger into her mouth again and twisted it around, getting it good and wet before focusing her attention on his other nipple.

"You think so, huh?" Alex croaked.

"Mmm. You analyze things to death."

Okay, so he did do that. He liked to think it was a Greek trait. One wasn't raised knowing that the world's first great thinkers were Greek without feeling obligated to follow in the tradition.

But even as fire swept through his abdomen, Alex thought that his heritage wasn't the only thing behind his actions. When he was five he would take his weekly allowance down to Old Man Mano's corner store and spend half an hour trying to decide what he wanted to spend it on. Mano used to tell him that one day his head was going to explode from the effort it took for him to buy a piece of nickel candy.

The only thing in his life he hadn't been hesitant about was his decision to go into law enforcement, then take the position as an insurance investigator.

Nicole wiggled her bottom so that she was closer to the area most in need of her attention. Alex's hips involuntarily bucked from the mattress. She laughed quietly as she rerouted her damp finger to the middle of his chest then slowly drew it down his stomach. Alex drew in a ragged breath and he trembled at the power of the tension growing inside his body. Not just in his groin, but all over. He was afraid that if he held his hand out he'd find it trembling.

"Nicole…"

She brushed her glorious hair to the other side of her face, sweeping the fresh-smelling, silken strands across his bare skin. He caught his breath, mesmerized. "Hmm?"

"Is your real name even Nicole?"

She gazed at him. "No."

"What is it?"

"If I told you then I'd have to kill you."

He started to chuckle then stopped as she tucked her finger into the waistband of his boxers and slowly tugged the material down until his erection sprang free. With the same finger, she began drawing lazy circles against his inflamed skin. He threw his head back against the pillow and gritted his teeth.

He heard her small intake of breath. "Mmm…wow."

"Hmm?" He was finding it increasingly difficult to concentrate on verbal conversation, but her comment intrigued him.

"Had many complaints?" she whispered.

He didn't understand. "Complaints?"

"About how…big you are."

He watched as she wrapped her fingers around the width of his erection, covering the knob of his arousal, then drawing her hand down over the length of him.

He honestly didn't know how he compared to other men. He'd never been the type to engage in that kind of one-upmanship. And none of the women he'd been with up until now had mentioned anything about his size.

"You look good enough to eat," she whispered.

Oh, yes, Alex thought in anticipation, pulling on the handcuffs, the thought of her wet, naughty mouth moving over him sending his blood pounding through his veins.

She bent over him, her hair trailing over his thighs as she flicked her pink tongue over the top of his arousal, then curved it partially around the width, her fingers tightly holding the base.

She slid her lips over the shiny dome and moved down over him, nearly sending him into cardiac arrest as her gaze rested solidly on his face, watching for his reaction.

Sweet Jesus, but she had an incredible mouth.

The hot texture of her tongue against his sensitive skin, the slick suction she applied and the squeezing of her fingers combined to send flames licking over every inch of his body.

Then just like that, her mouth and hand were gone.

Alex groaned, feeling his wrist growing raw from where he kept yanking on the cuffs. It was pure torture not to be able to touch her, not to be able to take control. Instead he was forced to lie back as she stripped off her skimpy panties then sat back down on his thighs, her skin nearly searing his.

He'd never seen a shaven pubis before up close and personal. There wasn't a lick of hair on her swollen flesh, nothing to impede his view of her engorged womanhood. And he found he'd very much like to return the favor of oral sex.

But all thoughts of that flew from his mind as she tore open a plastic packet then slowly, meticulously began rolling a condom down over him. Her dark eyes looked even darker as she finished rolling the lubricated latex down.

She scooted until her thighs rested on either side of

his hips. He groaned. Finally, finally, she was close enough to touch. And he did. Running his fingertips down the line of her swollen folds, he lightly dipped them into her wetness, then drew them up again, gently parting her to his sight.

Beautiful...

He heard her gasp as he flicked his thumb over her fleshy core. Then she was moving his hand away and maneuvering herself so that her bare womanhood hovered mere millimeters above his ramrod-straight erection.

Then she was moving down over him.

Shockwaves rushed through Alex. So tight. So wet. So...mind-blowingly phenomenal.

He grasped the flesh of her hip with his free hand and held her still for a long moment, reveling in the feel of being buried deep within her. In the sweet sensation of Nicole Bennett connected to him in the most intimate way.

She made a tiny sound of frustration. "Too slow," she murmured.

He blinked his eyes open to see what she was talking about, only to close them again as she began moving, stroking him with her slick flesh.

Alex groaned as the momentum of her movements increased, then watched as her hands joined his above his head, her bottom slapping against his thighs as she rode him as if he were a galloping horse and she the jockey intent on pushing him to the finish line first. Her face was drawn in utter concentration, her gaze firmly on his as she went down again and again, her breasts swaying, her heat growing hotter still.

His mouth watered with the desire to pull one of

those breasts in his mouth even as his blood steam-rolled through his veins. The sound of flesh against flesh, harsh, labored breathing and his own quickening heartbeat filled his ears. Then Nicole moaned.

The sound was soul deep and long, and wound around and around him, urging him toward a conclusion he didn't want to reach yet. He stiffened and his hips bucked upward violently. Seeming to catch on to his condition, Nicole instantly removed her heat and sat back, staring at him in the dim light.

Alex stopped breathing altogether as she grinned at him wickedly.

"A lesser woman might, um, leave you hanging. Pay you back for having kidnapped me last night," she whispered, appearing to have trouble finding air to fill her lungs with.

Alex yanked so hard on the cuffs he was afraid he'd dislodge the headboard and the bed would collapse beneath them. "But you won't," he said quietly.

She remained silent for a long moment, then shook her head. "Oh, no." She slid the earring from her left ear, then within ten seconds flat had unlocked the cuffs binding him. "I want to see if my theory's correct."

The words drifted through Alex's mind, but didn't register as he tackled her, pinning her against the other end of the mattress. She gasped, then giggled, then moaned as he pulled each of her breasts deep into his mouth and curved his hand down over her hip and under her bottom, parting her further.

"Mmm, I guess—"

The rest of her sentence exited on a ragged breath as Alex filled her.

In his entire life, he couldn't remember a time when

he felt this way. He was consumed by his need for this enigmatic woman. This woman who alternately teased him and surprised him. This woman who stoked his passion to such a fevered pitch he wondered if he was too turned on to come.

He slid into her to the hilt, then stopped.

She made a sound of frustration. "Please…"

"What's your theory?" he asked, her words a moment ago finally taking root.

She smiled up at him shakily, then smoothed her palms against his jaw. "That once all pretense is stripped away, we're very much alike, you and I." She swallowed hard, drawing his gaze down the length of her long neck to where sweat coated the skin of her chest. "What we feel, we feel strongly." She moved her hands to his buttocks. "And when we have sex, it's with no holds barred."

She ground her hips hungrily against his.

Alex groaned then drove into her like nobody's business, unsure how he felt about her words but knowing one thing as he dove for home. Sex with Nicole Bennett was out of this world.

THREE HOURS LATER Nicole lay across the width of the mattress, stark naked, watching the sky outside the tall windows begin to lighten, the first birds offering up tentative calls. She was soaked with sweat, completely sated and wishing the loft had central air to help her cool off.

"Summer's my favorite time of year," Alex said quietly from where he lay next to her staring at the same sight.

Nicole turned her head to look at him. "Yeah? Mine,

too." She looked at the sky again. "That and winter. You can have spring and fall. Too tame for me. I like the extremes."

She felt his gaze on her, but didn't acknowledge it.

She was happy that her theory about the uptight Alex Cassavetes had been correct. In her twenty-eight years she'd come to understand that most people lived behind various types of masks. The skill lay in looking beyond those masks and seeing the people underneath. She'd sensed from the first time she'd laid eyes on Alex outside that Baltimore pub, then later when he'd knocked on her door instead of going into his own room, that he was a man just itching to step outside of his stale box. That he was a man capable of great passion and fantastic sex.

Still, not even she had been prepared for his stamina, his sheer strength of will, that allowed him to hold off his own climax so that he could give her orgasm after glorious orgasm. It made sense that someone in law enforcement would value control. She'd had no idea that control could manifest itself in such a way, though. She couldn't remember a time when she'd gone that long with a guy. Couldn't remember when she'd felt her thighs ache, her stomach tremble, her limbs go limp from overactivity.

"Water," he said. "I need some water."

Nicole opened her mouth to ask him to bring her some, too, but was surprised when no sound came out.

Wow.

Imagine. Her. Rendered completely speechless.

She shifted slightly and squeezed her thighs together, causing a shudder to travel over her skin.

"Open," Alex said, blocking her view of the morning sky then nudging her feet with his knee.

She squinted at him then stretched one foot until it rested on the side of his knee, positioning herself so that she lay wide open to him.

He pressed a cold, hard water bottle against the swollen, overheated flesh between her legs. She gasped and came up off the bed, both shocked and turned on by the unexpected move. Alex grinned as he uncapped the bottle then took a long drink from it.

Nicole licked her lips, waiting for him to offer her some. He didn't. Instead he motioned her hand away and gestured that he'd like to hold the bottle for her.

Nicole lifted herself to her elbows with some effort and pursed her lips. He put the bottle to her mouth then tipped it. Half the cold liquid trickled down her chin onto her chest. He removed the bottle then joined her on the bed, licking the cool liquid from her skin, including her aching nipples.

After a few moments, he collapsed back to the mattress next to her. Nicole smiled. "At least you were able to get up and get water. I don't think I could move if I tried."

Alex stared at the ceiling. Nicole turned her gaze to the sky outside the windows. A girl could get used to this view.

"My mother used to say that you could tell what kind of day it was going to be from the sunrise," she said quietly.

She heard Alex shift but he didn't say anything.

"Unfortunately I never paid close attention, so I can't remember much of how, exactly, you went about doing that." She looked down at her chest, feeling a sudden, inexplicable desire to cover herself.

"Red sky at morning, sailors take warning. Red sky at night, sailor's delight," Alex said, reaching over her and tugging the sheet to partially cover them both across the hips. "My *yiayia* used to say that. I guess it's an old fishermen's saying."

Nicole pulled the sheet up to cover her breasts.

"Does your mother live in the city?" he asked.

"My mother doesn't live anywhere. She's dead."

A pause, then, "I'm sorry."

She swallowed and rested her hands on her stomach. "Don't be. You didn't kill her."

"She was murdered?"

"Yes. By cancer."

She fell silent, remembering the apartment in Brooklyn Heights where she and her family used to live. How, day by day, her mother grew weaker. Lost her hair during chemotherapy sessions. But not even a disease like cancer could keep her down. She was always smiling. Always asking her and Jeremy questions, reading to them at night, as if she was trying to cram a lifetime's worth of love into a few short months.

"I was seven when she died," she found herself saying. "My brother and I just came home from school one day to find her gone. No hospital visits. She was just gone."

She lay there, a part of her surprised she had shared what she had. Another waiting for Alex's response.

"What did she look like?" he murmured.

In all her imaginings, she would never have guessed he'd ask that. She rolled onto her side and gazed at him, her head propped up on her elbow. Then she smiled. "Beautiful. She had this soft brown hair. And big blue eyes that sparkled when she laughed." She moved her hand to rest against his chest. "She used to love going for long walks. We'd leave Jeremy home with my father and she and I would walk up and down the street, talking to the neighbors, asking the butcher how his wife was doing, the bookstore owner what was new on the shelves." She sighed softly.

"It must have been hard losing her at such a young age."

Nicole lay her head against her arm and idly moved her fingertips over his chest. "It wasn't easy."

She remembered months of silence, her father's long absences when the neighbor would come to look after her and her brother. Then, finally, the curtain had seemed to lift and she and Jeremy learned what their father did for a living. He wasn't a used-car salesman like the guy across the street. Or a stockbroker like Johnny's father down the block. He was a thief.

And it wasn't long after that that she and Jeremy had found themselves following in their father's footsteps.

There had never been a time when guilt was associated with what they were doing. Oh, they'd known it was illegal. And that if you got caught, you got in trouble. But their father had carefully begun to school them. Where other families went to Central Park for picnics, they'd gone under the guise of sharing a picnic, when what they were really doing was practicing for what would come later. A filched picnic basket here. A borrowed set of car keys there. They'd always given the items back in a way that didn't implicate them. After all, their father explained, these were practice runs, not the real thing. When you did the real thing, you went for larger items. Like pricey antiques, which were what he targeted.

"And your brother?"

Nicole blinked to stare at Alex. Had she really just said all that aloud? Really shared with him what she had never told another individual? She felt suddenly antsy, uncomfortable.

Alex curved an arm under her head and pulled her closer.

"Anyway," she said, reaching for the water bottle. "Enough about my boring life. Tell me about your family."

She made the mistake of meeting his gaze as she swallowed water. The intense, questioning expression on his face made her heart beat a little faster.

"Are you sure you want to hear it?" he asked, grinning.

She settled back in next to him, her hand idly reaching for his groin. "Oh, yeah. I want to hear everything that went into making this virtual sex machine."

He chuckled. "There will be plenty of time for that later," he said and turned her over onto her back, letting her know exactly what he had in mind for now.

And Nicole wasn't about to argue with him....

7

MUCH LATER that morning, Nicole sat alone sipping
latte at a restaurant across the street from the auction
house. There, they would sell off the collection of valu-
able paintings to the highest bidder in four days. Despite the fact that she'd gotten very little sleep last
night she felt energized, refreshed, her muscles seeming to sing a tune she couldn't quite place but she
hummed to anyway.

She took a long pull off her latte then leisurely licked
the foam off her top lip. Amazing what a little great sex
could accomplish.

A little? She propped her elbow on the table then
planted her chin in her hand. Alex would have
knocked her socks off had she been wearing any. As it
stood, nearly every muscle in her body ached, her
thighs still felt on fire and she was sitting there thinking about how very hard it had been to leave him
sleeping a few hours ago. Especially when she knew a
couple of light, naughty touches could get a rise out of
him while he was still asleep.

Someone sighed. With a start, she realized it was her.

She snapped upright. She never sighed. At least not
in that wistful, first-blush way. It was just something
she didn't do. Not as a high school freshman when
she'd set her sights on the senior captain of the varsity
football team. Not even when she thought she was in

love about five years back when she'd hooked up with
a French sculptor who'd known exactly what to do
with his hands. Sighing just wasn't something she was
given to doing. Not in exasperation. Not in disgust.
And certainly not in a mushy, longing way that made
her seem like a dreamy-eyed idiot.

Okay, so the sex was good. No, great. No, incredible.
She waved her hand at her own inability to settle on a
word then picked up her oversize cup again. So what?
Sex was sex, no matter how incredible. She'd just happened to meet up with a guy who knew how to do it
right, that's all. Well, with a little instruction, anyway.
Alex's habit of trying to slow things down all the time
frustrated her to no end. She liked it fast and rough.
And, oh boy, had he proven the right man for the job.

But if sex was sex, what was she doing sitting there
wondering what he was doing right now? And smiling
at the knowledge that he was probably climbing the
walls wondering where she was and when she'd be
back?

She was a woman used to coming and going as she
wished. No explanations. No set time for meeting up.
Nobody to account to for her actions. Of course, since
her mother had died, no one had really asked her to do
any of that, either.

Strange...

A delivery truck pulled up outside the auction
house. She sat back and opened the newspaper she'd
brought along, pretending an interest in the sports section as she watched the driver get out and go inside.
Minutes later he came back out again with a well-
dressed older man, a guy she had already pegged as
one of the partners of the auction house.

She'd learned from one of the part-time auction house stock workers that a few of the less expensive pieces had been delivered days ago and were sitting in the house's basement vault. Amazing what a nice, crisp one hundred dollar bill could accomplish, especially when the information needed was essentially nonthreatening. After all, how could sharing information on what had already been delivered and placed under tight security endanger the pieces themselves?

But these pieces here...they were the real deal. If the hands-on presence of the auction house partner wasn't a clear indication, then the Brinks-like security of the truck, and the uniformed men that climbed out of the back door, were.

Personally, she tended to stay away from anything with a lock on it. Technology today was ever evolving and hard to keep up with. Learn how to crack one safe, and the next day the mechanism changed and you were scrambling to learn how to bypass that one. Gone were the days when a couple of sticks of dynamite or plastique would do the job. Anyway, all that was too messy for her.

She watched the men carry pieces one by one from the truck into the auction house at the same time that she turned the page of the paper, then reached for an almond biscotti and dipped it into her latte.

She preferred crimes that required a little more finesse, a little role-playing, and, preferably, someone else to do the job for her without their knowing.

She crunched on the Italian breakfast biscuit then scanned the newspaper, zooming in on an ad for the auction house and its pricey stock up for bid next Tuesday morning.

She slid her cell phone from her purse and dialed Alex's business number. She was immediately put through to his office by his secretary, who apparently would never forget her. She smiled.

"Cassavetes."

Nicole's smile widened. Her own personal Greek god. Her own Alexander the Greatest. "Hey," she murmured.

He didn't say anything right away.

She cleared her throat. "I didn't get a chance to ask you last night—" namely because they'd been busy with other business "—did you go ahead and work up that faux policy you were talking about?"

"Funny you should ask. I'm holding a copy of it in my hands right now."

"And it's making the rounds?"

"Faster than a speeding bullet."

She took a long sip of latte. "Good, that means you have time on your hands...."

On the other end of the phone, Alex paused and sat back in his chair, the springs squeaking. "Depends on what you mean by time."

And it also depended on what she had in mind. If she was going to suggest they head back to his apartment for what would amount to his first "nooner," he was all for it.

He glanced down at the front of his slacks then snapped immediately upright in his chair, nearly injuring himself in the process.

He didn't know what it was, but all Nicole had to do was blink and he was hard. He grimaced, realizing she couldn't exactly do that over the phone. But he could hear the smile in her voice. And that alone made him want her.

"I mean, can you get out of the office?"

Alex grinned. "Oh, yeah." He craned his neck to glance out his open door at where his secretary pretended not to be listening to his end of the conversation. He swiveled his chair to face his window. "What did you have in mind?"

"Possibility number two."

He squinted. Were those people in the office building across the street staring at him? Or was he getting paranoid in his old age? "I don't get you."

"The policy I chose that was taken out by the auction house? I'm sitting across the street from the house in question now. The prize pieces are being delivered as we speak."

Alex's ego deflated like a helium balloon.

"You won't regret it. This restaurant serves great biscotti."

He turned back toward his desk and tried not to let her hear his disappointment. "No thanks. I've got a meeting at one with my superior. Considering I was a no-show at the last two, I have to be there."

Silence.

Alex rubbed the bridge of his nose, then turned to the page in the faux policy that mentioned the uncirculated Double Eagle ten-dollar coins.

"Nicole?"

"I'm still here." It sounded like she was drinking something. "You really think he's going to go for the coins, don't you?"

"If you mean do I think you're wasting your time at the auction house? Yes, I do."

His loft was another matter entirely. Hell, he'd even be willing to risk his boss's wrath if she so much as hinted at wanting to return there.

"Okay. It's your funeral."

Not exactly the imagery running through his mind just then. "Funeral?"

"Yeah. You know, for your job." She crunched into something, then hummed as she chewed. Alex swallowed hard. "D.M. is not going for the metal, Alex. He's going to hit the auction house. Probably four days from now, on the night before the auction."

"How do you know that?"

"Gut instinct."

And what a gut she had, too.

"Isn't that the reason you kidnapped me in Baltimore? Because of my ability to sniff these things out?"

He blew a long breath through his lips. "I didn't kidnap you. I apprehended you. And you are now officially my informer."

"I'm nobody's stoolie, Alex."

Oh, how he knew that.

"I've got to go."

There was a sudden urgency in her voice and Alex tensed. "What is it?"

"I think I just spotted somebody I recognize." He heard rustling paper.

"Hey—" Alex said, afraid she'd already hung up.

"What?" she said quietly, moments later.

He grinned. "What time will I see you back at my place?"

She didn't answer right away. Something he didn't like at all.

"Goodbye, Alex."

He opened his mouth to object, but quickly realized that she'd already hung up.

He dropped the receiver into its cradle then leaned back in his chair again. Had she really spotted someone? Or had it been an excuse? And why in the hell couldn't she answer a simple question? It was normal for a guy to want to see the woman he'd just had incredible sex with, wasn't it?

Unless it hadn't been incredible for her.

He groaned.

"Can I get you something, Mr. Cassavetes?"

"Yes, a psychiatrist. I need my head examined."

"Excuse me?"

"Nothing, Dorothy. I don't need anything. Thanks for asking."

At least he didn't need anything from *her*. Not unless she could offer up some advice on how to handle a woman who didn't adhere to traditional rules, either in life or dating.

Were they dating?

He watched Dorothy leave the room.

"Close the door, please," he called after her.

She stared at him, puzzled, then did what he asked.

Last night there had emerged a moment that felt...traditional somehow. Real. Two people connecting on both a physical and an emotional plane.

No one could have been more surprised than him when she'd offered up the information about her mother. Even she'd seemed stunned that she'd said the words, as if she hadn't been aware she'd spoken them out loud. Hearing her experiences had made him feel awkward and sympathetic and fiercely protective of her. Which was the last thing he wanted.

Damn it, she was a thief. She stole things that he tried to recover. She followed a completely different code of ethics. She was completely without morals....

He felt himself go hot all over again.

Oh, how completely without morals she was....

He shook his head to clear it. This was insane. Crazy.

His gaze settled on his in-box and the cases waiting there to be investigated, then the pile on the other side of his desk on the policies issued over the past two months. He reached for that pile and started leafing through them, wondering if she was right about D.M.

His eye caught on something in one of the files. More specifically, a policy that was written up a week ago for a full and very expensive set of Tiffany jewelry. He closed the file and noted how far it was down from the top. Near the bottom. Had Nicole seen it and purposely placed it at the bottom of the stack to make it look like she hadn't seen it? Or had she genuinely not gotten that far?

Why was he getting the feeling that he should be a little more careful with her?

Damn.

IT HAD BEEN A WHILE since Nicole had worn a maid's uniform. Specifically over a year ago when she'd impersonated a maid at Christine Bowman's rented house in St. Louis.

She braced herself as the taxi made a sharp right on Broadway, then adjusted her short black wig with the aid of her compact mirror. Oh, what a score that had been. She smiled, then wiped a bit of lipstick from the corner of her mouth. A tidy sum in uncut diamonds. And her plan had gone like clockwork, up to and including Christine Bowman's arrest for the crime after Nicole had already lifted the diamonds.

She clapped her compact closed and slid it into her black leather backpack. The other day Alex had asked her if she was somehow violating the code of honor among thieves by targeting other thieves. She sat back and stared blindly through the window. A light summer rain had begun falling a little while after she'd left her post at the auction house and it made everything look blurry, dim. It had been a long time since she'd given a great deal of thought to what she did. A long time since she'd bothered to remember why and when she'd decided to target other thieves rather than make her own direct scores. And she wasn't altogether sure she wanted to think about it now.

She tugged on the white collar of the black-and-white starched maid's uniform. She'd been nineteen and become the unwitting victim of another thief. She'd just lifted her second set of Tiffany jewelry—a classic canary-yellow diamond set of necklace, bracelet and ring—when she'd gotten hit outside the house from where she'd taken it. Only there had been no flair in the second stealing. The thief, one of her father's old cronies, had nearly killed her when she'd fought against him. She remembered the wild look on his face as he'd stared at her. The soulless shadows in his eyes as he held up a lead pipe and beat her to within an inch of her life.

She'd spent five days in the county hospital cramped in the same room with other uninsured unfortunates. Gunshot victims, victims of gang stabbings, people who attempted suicide, crack mothers. And while she'd always been street-smart, she'd never spent a great deal of time on that particular part of the street. And she'd realized as she'd gotten to know each and every one of her fellow patients that all of them were victims of another criminal. That just as there were cold-hearted crooks that sat behind CEO desks in large conglomerates taking from the less fortunate, so there were people in her profession that preyed on their own and were just as unlikely to be punished for their crimes.

So she'd set out to punish them.

She'd been young enough then to think of herself as The Equalizer. The Robin Hood of Manhattan, who stole from the undeserving thieves and gave back to those who had been hurt.

And in the case of D.M., increasingly those people were the families of those he killed.

She shuddered then rolled down her window, uncaring that rain got inside. She needed the air, needed to warm the air-conditioned air inside the cab.

"Hey, lady, you mind? You're ruining my seats," the cabby complained.

She asked him to turn down the air then rolled the window back up. That was okay. They were coming up to her drop-off point anyway. She reached into her backpack, pushed aside the small caliber gun she'd recovered from Alex's loft, then pulled out her fake bonded card to flash at the head housekeeper she'd talked to on the phone earlier.

The cab pulled over to stop at the curb and she stuffed money into the Plexiglas drawer, staring at the upscale apartment building as she waited for her change.

The lady of the house was at a charity luncheon that

would stretch well into the dinner hour. Her husband, undoubtedly, would be at work, just like all husbands that lived in this neighborhood. It was more than that they merely needed the money to cover the overhead, but men of this type tended to either be workaholics or had other interests that didn't involve their wife or home.

That meant that only the housekeeping staff would be on hand—the head housekeeper who had answered the phone and perhaps one or two others.

She collected her change and left a large tip. "You didn't see me," she said.

The cabby grinned at her in the rearview mirror as he pocketed the money. "So long as you don't kill anybody, we're copasetic."

She climbed out of the cab and waited until it rolled away.

The doorman stood looking at her warily from the double glass doors. She smiled at him then cleared her throat. When he smiled back, she knew she wouldn't have any trouble blowing by him, and she didn't. She had to fake a French accent, broken English and a twisted ankle along with a sob story about needing this job to cover her mother's medical bills, but he was a breeze compared to other doormen. She'd encountered her share that wouldn't let her in no matter what. If you weren't on the visitor's list, and the person in charge didn't approve your being buzzed up, then you were out of luck, left scurrying for an alternative access to the premises. That's usually where she called things off. When you started scaling fire escapes and busting windows, you were just begging to be caught and arrested.

The housekeeper, however, was another story.

Nicole stood in the third-floor hallway, calculating her odds of getting inside. She didn't even try smiling at the matronly-looking Hispanic who looked like she wouldn't let Guiliani himself in to use the bathroom. She merely handed over her fake bonded card, started mumbling about needing to get this job over with, and forced her way inside the apartment.

"*Señora, señora,*" the housekeeper called after her, following her down the main hall. "I must talk to the lady of the house before I let you in here."

The key to success in any job was quickness. Nicole turned, held her hand palm out and began bobbing her head in exasperation the way she'd seen a Puerto Rican friend do. "Don't '*señora*' me. I've been stuck in traffic for the past hour, lady, and had to pay a fortune in cab fare to get here because 'the lady of the house' demanded someone be sent here pronto." She turned and continued walking, hoping the design of the two-floor apartment was standard. "It was my friggin' day off. And now I gotta pee something terrible."

There. There was the guest bathroom. Right where it usually was, tucked away neatly under the staircase.

The housekeeper was on her heels. Nicole turned and did the palm-out thing again. "Don't even think about following me in there. I won't be responsible for what I'll do."

The older woman looked shocked at the possibility that physical violence might be involved. She backed up then hurried in the other direction. Probably to get whomever else was in the house.

Nicole closed and locked the bathroom door, then

glanced at her watch. Three minutes. Not bad. Not a record or anything, but nothing to cough at.

She put her bag down then flipped open the lid to the commode. There wasn't much toilet paper on the roll so she found another one under the sink and began rolling it around her open hand. Judging the wad to be thick enough for the old plumbing systems of these apartments, she put the half-empty roll back under the sink then stuck her hand with the wad in it into the toilet. She hated this part, but hey, with any luck the bowl had been cleaned that morning. She stepped to the sink and washed up then waited.

She didn't have to wait long. A few seconds later there came the expected banging at the door. "*Señora,* you muss pleeeaze come out now."

I'd like nothing better.

Nicole made sure her wig was straight then reached over to flush the toilet. As designed the wad stopped it up and water began cascading over the top. She grabbed her pack then opened the door, feigning horror.

"Oh, no! Look what's happened! What am I going to do?"

An elderly man stood with the housekeeper. Her husband? She suspected so.

Nicole stood back to allow them to enter the confined space then peered out into the hallway. No one else was in sight.

"The mop," she said. "Where's the friggin' mop?"

The couple was trying to stop the flow.

"In zee kitchen pantry!" the housekeeper shouted. "It's in zee pantry!"

Nicole rushed out into the hall…then closed them in.

There was the simple matter of shoving the stopper under the door and she was free and clear. At least for the next five or so minutes.

She rushed up the stairs to the second floor, searching for the master bedroom where Nessbaum would have the jewels stashed. Guest room...guest room... master bedroom!

She paused briefly in the doorway, then rushed in.

With the click-click of an internal clock mingling with the sound of the housekeeper and her husband pounding on the downstairs bathroom door, she made her way to the walk-in closet, pushed aside the shoes lined up there, then pulled up the loose carpet.

Bingo.

There in a simple, easily breached lockbox, was the newly purchased Elsa Peretti-designed Tiffany jewelry in its original case.

"You really need to invest in a proper safe, Mrs. Nessbaum," she could virtually hear the police telling the woman when she returned home to find her new treasures missing.

Ignoring the other significant pieces of jewelry—and there were several large-carat diamonds set in platinum and gold, along with a significant set of large black pearls—she slid the ones she was after into her own velvet pouch and pulled the silk cord.

Done.

She hurried downstairs, sparing a sympathetic glance toward the blocked bathroom door. She'd call and alert the doorman from a cab a couple of blocks away. She pressed the elevator button and glanced at her watch. Eight minutes from doorway to doorway. She smiled. Not bad. Not her best time, but not bad.

And in five days Mrs. Nessbaum would find her jewelry sitting in her mailbox, cleaned, still in its original box and as good as new along with a small thank you card bearing no clues as to Nicole's identity.

Thankfully the doorman was helping an elderly woman bring in her many afternoon purchases. She spared him a wave, then stepped quickly up the sidewalk and around the corner where she lifted her hand for a taxi.

One pulled up from where it had been parked across the street. She climbed in. She gave the driver an address, then turned to stare at the man seated next to her. She gasped.

"Get the jewelry?" Alex asked, wearing a wicked grin.

A SHORT BLACK WIG.

Alex's gaze traveled over Nicole's maid's uniform, thinking he would have preferred something a little more risqué. Something shorter, significantly tighter, with one of those skirts that had layers and layers of white lace underneath. But he could see where this would get the job done better.

Where did she get all this stuff?

"I don't know what you're talking about," she murmured as the taxi pulled away from the curb and merged with the thick Manhattan traffic.

"Mmm." Alex crossed his arms over his chest. "What? I'm supposed to believe maid service is your day job?"

The smile she gave him was by no means plain and unassuming. It was downright filthy and came very close to erasing the entire reason he'd left his office a half hour ago and headed straight to the east-side residence. The reason being to confirm or disprove his suspicions, he reminded himself.

"Sure, why not? What, do you believe I think cleaning houses is beneath me?"

Alex wished *he* was beneath her. Namely lying across his bed, her firm, hot bottom bouncing against his thighs.

There must have been something in his eyes that gave away his thoughts because she relaxed against the seat of the cab and hiked up the long skirt of her uniform until the hem rested high on her thighs. With great, calculated flair, she crossed her legs. It was then he realized she had on fishnet stockings.

His gaze flicked back up to her short wig. She twirled a silken strand around her index finger, then pulled it until she could suck on the end in a joltingly provocative way. With her other hand, she slowly unbuttoned the neck of the uniform, then tucked the material back until he could see the soft, tantalizing swells of her breasts in a red push-up bra.

The taxi swerved and Alex moved to anchor himself. A glance toward the driver told him what he suspected. That the cabbie was watching Nicole as closely as he was.

He knocked on the Plexiglas separation. "Hey, watch the road, buddy!"

Not that he thought the driver would respect his request. A babe like Nicole climbed into the back of your taxi, you were bound to pay attention. Especially when she was offering up a primo show.

Nicole's husky laugh tugged Alex's attention back to her.

He held out his hand, palm up. "Cough it up."

She blinked at him in mock innocence. "Pardonez moi?"

Mmm, French. The whole maid routine was beginning to grow roots in the dirty fantasy section of his mind.

He dropped his hand, but instead of to the seat, he cupped a slender knee. He enjoyed her small gasp of surprise. "The jewels, Nic."

Her eyes were pure seduction. "I can think of some other jewels I'd rather give you."

The taxi swerved again, this time earning the beeps of countless shrill horns.

Alex took his hand away then settled back into his seat. "Play it the way you want, Nicole. But know this. During the time we're working together? You do not steal from any of my company's clients." He leveled a stare at her. "You do not steal, period, do you hear me?"

She dropped all pretence and made a face. "Or what?"

"Or else I haul your cute little ass to jail."

8

TWO DAYS LATER Alex was no closer to gaining control over Nicole Bennett. Worse, he increasingly felt as if he were on some sort of slippery emotional slope leading to Lord only knew where.

He glanced out the taxi window at the passing businesses on Queens Boulevard, a familiar ride. Living in Manhattan, he didn't own a car and didn't have to, given the city's transit system. But sometimes, like today, he idly thought about getting one.

It was hard to believe it was Sunday already. In fact, recently he'd found it hard to believe it was any day like it had been a week before. Friday no longer seemed like a normal, run-of-the-mill Friday, and after having a little—okay, a lot—of unplanned nookie this morning, Sunday certainly didn't seem like Sunday. Oh, yeah, traffic was lighter. It was the only day of the week when life seemed to slow down a bit in Manhattan, and more significantly in the surrounding boroughs, giving the manmade stretch of steel and concrete a sci-fi futuristic feel. In a city of seven million, it wasn't unusual to wonder where they all were on a Sunday.

He covered his face with his hands, almost swearing he could still smell Nicole's sweet, musky scent on his fingers even though he'd had a shower after finally crawling his way out of bed and leaving her to sleep an hour ago. The differences between how he'd viewed life before last Wednesday and how he viewed it now were many. He didn't need that cup of coffee anymore to wake up in the morning. Instead he got up in full throttle, ready to take on anything that came his way. Instead of scheduling for a central-air system to be installed in his loft, he found he enjoyed the feel of the rising temperatures. Liked lying in bed with Nicole all sweaty and hot and sated, nothing but the warm summer breeze blowing in the window and an old rattling fan to cool them.

He'd never found the jewelry.

He remembered their encounter two days ago in the back of the taxi, the same day he'd looked through the files holding recently issued policies and the one for the Tiffany jewelry had jumped out at him. He'd known with every instinct he had that she'd go after it. And when he'd gone by the auction house as she'd requested to find her gone, he'd decided to check out the Nessbaum place. He'd been surprised and disappointed when she'd stepped onto the street in the maid's uniform, having already completed the job.

Oh, he knew she had the jewelry stashed somewhere. He just hadn't been able to figure out where.

There were a lot of things he hadn't been able to figure out yet.

He already knew that she didn't call any one place home. And after that first time they'd had sex and she'd allowed him a glimpse into her life, she'd quietly closed that door again, smiling at his questions, distracting him with her hot little body.

Hey, he wasn't complaining.

Much.

He found himself grinning. Oh, he used to wonder about men who allowed women to keep them. He'd watched friends from college go from player status to married sap overnight. But only now did he remotely understand why they had done what they had. It wasn't something he could verbally explain. Hell, *he* wasn't sure what was happening. But it was like someone, namely Nicole, had flipped a switch on inside him. A switch that repeated over and over again some kind of subliminal mantra. "You only want me, you only want me. You can't stop thinking about me. You can't stop wanting me, wanting me..."

Damned if he knew where the switch was. And even if he did, would he want to shut it off?

There was something exhilarating about being under Nicole's spell. A flicker of the unknown. It had made him realize that he'd gotten used to life the way it was, the day-in-day-out daily grind, that he always felt like he'd been there, done everything. Then there was her and—*bam!*—everything changed. Everything was new again. Unfamiliar. Exciting.

He tapped on the window. "You can let me out anywhere to the right here," he told the cabby. He peeled off the amount of the fare and a tip, then climbed from the taxi, barely aware that it drove off as he stared at his parents' house.

He'd grown up here, on this quiet residential street with its old trees and neat lawns lined one up against the other. The first eighteen years of his life he'd known the three-bedroom house in Astoria as home. A place he couldn't wait to get out of when he was eighteen and he went off to university with a bunch of pals. A place he returned to nearly every Sunday for family dinner. His father's ten-year-old Caprice sat in the driveway, the only make of car he ever remembered Georgos Cassavetes owning. Every ten years he traded the old one in for a newer model, but the make remained the same. As did the navy-blue color.

Alex was surprised to find himself standing at the curb, hands in his slacks pockets, reminiscing about the house he'd grown up in.

He shook his head and walked up the driveway and let himself in the front door. The smell of cooking meat and the low sound of old Greek bouzouki music laced with clarinet drifted to him from the kitchen. He heard his mother's voice as she said something, then stepped into the room at the back of the house to find her shaking a wooden spoon at his sister where she sat sorting through fava beans at the pine table.

"You disappeared, Athena. For two whole days. Don't ever do that to your mother again. You want I should die an early death? I'm fifty-eight. Too young to die."

Athena acknowledged Alex with a smile, then rolled her eyes to stare at the ceiling. "Mama, I've been back home for three days now. Will you stop already?"

Helen Cassavetes had a white apron on that bore a needlepoint outline of the Acropolis across the bottom. She turned to shake her spoon at Athena again and spotted Alex.

"Mama," he said.

"And you!" She shook the spoon at him instead. "How often do I ask you to help me out? Never. And you didn't even call me back to find out your sister had come home."

Alex bent to place a kiss to his mother's cheek. "You

ask me for help all the time, Mama." He looked her over. "Have you gotten your hair done? You look especially pretty this morning."

She whacked him in the arm with the spoon, but the slight color staining her cheeks told him she was flattered by the compliment. "Don't give me that, you little *kolopetho.*"

Alex chuckled at the mild rebuke and leaned over her to lift the lid on the large pan simmering on the stove. "Mmm. Smells good."

"What, you expected it should smell bad?"

Alex hugged her, pausing for a moment to enjoy the moment.

While his family had always been affectionate, he realized he'd always taken the gestures for granted. But for this one moment he savored the feel of his mother. The first person who'd ever held him. He breathed in the familiar scent of the powder she always wore on her neck. Felt the warmth of her skin from cooking.

"What's wrong, *agapemou?*" she asked.

Alex grinned then kissed her on her still pretty cheek again. "Nothing." He released her. "Where's Papa?"

"Where else?" Athena replied, scooping the beans she'd sorted through into a clean pan then discarding the others. "In the backyard trying to teach Pericles to sit."

Pericles was a dog. A blond pointer fifteen years old if he was a day. And every Sunday morning like clockwork, his father would take him out into the backyard and try to teach him tricks. And Pericles would ignore him. Alex stepped to the back door and spotted his father moving a chew toy under the aging dog's nose then throw it.

"Fetch!" George called, pretending to throw the bone again.

Pericles dropped to a prone position at his feet, laid his head on top of his paws and gave a little whine.

"*Koproskilo*," his father called him a lazy dog in Greek, then patted Pericles's head.

Alex opened the door and stepped out onto the cement patio his father had laid himself twenty years ago.

"Alexanthros!" George got to his feet and Alex kissed him on his right cheek, his left, then his right again, bracing himself for the hearty pats on the back that always went along with the traditional greeting.

"Still trying to teach Pericles a few tricks, huh?"

"Sit, sit." His father motioned toward the chair next to his. "Damn dog. Not worth the food we feed him."

Alex nodded and patted the dog in question when Pericles put his head in Alex's lap. He knew his father's words were just that, words. The truth was Pericles and his father were like two old best friends, always together when his father was home. It was going to kill his dad when the old mutt passed away. Athena was already talking about getting a puppy to help ease the pain.

His mother appeared in the screen door. "Don't get too comfortable. Dinner will be ready in five minutes."

Alex sat back in his chair, enjoying the feel of the summer sun. His parents had probably gone to St. Demetrios Greek Orthodox Church for mass, and had likely dragged Athena there along with them if his sister's dress was any indication. As was tradition, they enjoyed a midafternoon dinner on Sunday. It was just after 2:00 p.m.

"I've been thinking about retiring," his father said, surprising him. "You know, selling George's Carry Out."

Alex stared at him. For as long as he could remember, the corner grocer had been his father's life. "Oh?" he said, uncertain what else he should say.

George grinned. "Yes." He motioned with his hand. "Your cousin Niko, the little upstart, came by the other day and offered to buy me out."

"What did you say?"

His father snorted. "I told him to get the hell out of my store."

Alex chuckled.

"But I've been thinking..." He trailed off.

Alex looked at him. Really looked at him for the first time in years.

Georgos Cassavetes was getting older and the years were beginning to show. His once jet-black hair was now almost completely white. The tiny wrinkles around his eyes and mouth were turning into deeper grooves. And if Alex wasn't mistaken, his father may have shrunk an inch or two over the years. Why hadn't he noticed that before?

"I've been thinking that your mom and I should return to Greece."

Alex nearly fell off his chair.

While they'd always tried to visit Greece at least every other year, he had never heard either one of his parents talk about moving back there permanently.

His father squinted at him. "You know, before we're too old to enjoy ourselves." He absently rubbed his left hand where recently he had complained of some joint pain. "I've been back and forth with a Realtor over there and there's a nice apartment outside Athens in Brahami. New. Affordable. Near where I grew up."

Alex cleared his throat. "And Mom? What does she think of all this?"

His father sighed and shrugged. "I don't know. I haven't said anything to her yet." He paused. "But she misses the place, you know?" He sat back. "We live our lives like we were still in Greece anyway. The way we eat. The friends we choose. Hell, we even watch all the Greek channels on the satellite over here."

Alex leaned forward and rested his forearms on his knees, trying to take in the news. If he found it ironic that his father's talk of changing everything came on the heels of his finally appreciating the sameness of their lives, he wasn't going to admit it.

"It's nice over there. Beautiful country."

"It doesn't suck here," Alex said.

His father smiled at him, then reached over to pat his knee. "No, it doesn't. But here doesn't have the waters of the Aegean. The beaches. Geez, I can't even buy a decent fish here, while there I could eat my choice of fresh fish every day."

"I'll bring you fish from the market in Manhattan."

A chuckle, then his father went silent.

"Alex?" his mother called.

He slowly tore his gaze away from his father to look at where she was standing on the other side of the screen door. She looked puzzled.

"You have a visitor," she said.

Alex frowned. A visitor? Who would be visiting him here?

He started to get up when the visitor in question

opened the back door and stepped outside. He nearly fell headfirst into the grass.

"Hi, Alex," Nicole said.

OKAY, MAYBE THIS hadn't been such a great idea.

Nicole fought the urge to toy with the wavy red wig she had on, and felt grossly underdressed in the tight faux leopard skin miniskirt, tiger-striped tank top and clunky costume jewelry she had on. She'd retrieved the tarty disguise from a Grand Central Station locker when she'd gone there to catch the train out to Astoria. Alex had told her that's where he'd be going, and it hadn't taken much to find the address. It was the first entry in the address book he kept in a drawer next to his kitchen phone.

Her bracelet of large wood beads held together by a thin black rope clanked as she nervously toyed with her hair. Maybe she should have gone with the girl-next-door look instead. Yes, the plain brown wig and the flowery sundress would have been much more appropriate.

She cleared her throat where the entire Cassavetes family stared at her, Alex included, and reminded herself that appropriate hadn't been what she was going for. She was aiming for chaos. She saw this as an opportunity to pay Alex back for ruining a perfectly good score the other day. And if her actions also pointed out to him that she would never be the type of woman he could take home to Mom...well, so much the better.

She swallowed hard. Only now that she was here and saw what a nice, normal family he had, she found herself wishing she could be that type of woman.

"Sorry I'm late, baby," she said, forging ahead with

the role she'd decided to play as she toddled over to Alex on her black stiletto heels and pressed a loud kiss to Alex's frozen mouth.

He looked like someone had just blindsided him with a two-by-four. Which, considering that had been her intention, was a good thing.

The older man she guessed to be his father coughed into his hand. "Aren't you going to introduce us, Alex?"

Alex looked like he was incapable of taking a breath just then. Nicole smiled at him, then turned and thrust her jewelry-laden hand at the elder Cassavetes. "Hi, I'm Nikki. Nikki Bennett. I'm sure Alex has told you all about me."

The younger woman gave a short laugh where she and her mother had come out onto the back patio with her. Nicole glanced at her, liking her on sight. There was an amused but curious expression on her face, but not a trace of harsh judgment.

The woman stepped forward. "Hi, I'm Athena. Alex's sister. It's nice to meet you, Nikki. Alex hasn't brought anyone home in ages. And apparently he leads a much more interesting life than we thought."

Nicole grinned. *Oh, yes*, she thought. *I definitely like her.*

"And you must be Mrs. Cassavetes. What a pleasure to meet you," Nicole said, having to pick up the woman's hand where it lay motionless at her side. She pumped it enthusiastically, wondering if she'd accidentally sent Alex's mother into cardiac arrest. She fought a frown. Definitely not what she wanted. In fact, she was a little disappointed to discover that she wished his mother would somehow see through her getup and find a way to like her.

Alex finally seemed to snap to as he grabbed Nicole by her upper arm. "If you'll excuse us a minute..."

He roughly steered Nicole toward the house. She fought to keep her balance on the ridiculous heels, reminded of why she preferred flats to these dangerous contraptions.

"Where are you taking me?" she asked as he guided her inside the house, through the kitchen and into the hall, showing no signs of stopping. She eyed the front door, half afraid he was going to throw her out. Instead he pushed her up the steps and into the middle bedroom on the second floor, then slammed the door closed.

Nicole looked around the room done in whites and neon blues, taking in the flag she guessed to be Greek that hung on the wall behind the single bed bearing a navy-blue bedspread.

She turned to face Alex and felt a little jolt of fear. He looked angrier than anyone she'd seen in her life.

"What in the hell are you doing here? And why in the hell are you dressed like that?"

ALEX WATCHED Nicole spread her arms wide and smile. "Surprise!"

Oh, he was surprised, all right. And majorly pissed.

Alex paced back and forth across his childhood bedroom, trying to reign in his anger. He'd come so close to throwing her taut-looking butt out of the house it was scary. He slanted a glance at her, taking in her tight skirt, the way she was all but falling out of her top and the sexy red hair...and felt the incredible desire to tackle her to the twin bed behind her and have sex with her in those slutty shoes.

He stopped in the middle of the room and closed his eyes, cursing up a blue streak in Greek.

When he opened his eyes again, Nicole was smiling at him, a cocky hand on her hip. For God's sake, she looked like a five-dollar whore. And she had come to his parents' house looking that way. Purposely. He shook his head, unable to grasp her motivation.

He forced himself to stare past her at the wall full of certificates and shelves of trophies. He motioned with his hand. "Talk."

He swallowed hard, discovering that even her choice of perfumes was over the top, yet oddly appealing.

"Hmm. When you closed the door, I didn't think talking was what you had in mind."

No, murdering her was closer to what he wanted to do.

But now...

Oh, the hell with it.

Alex grabbed her wrist and tossed her to the bed, then launched himself on top of her. Instantly she spread her thighs and curved her legs around his back. He swore savagely then kissed her. Angrily. Hungrily. One hand groping for her luscious breasts, the other diving to see if she was wearing any panties.

She wasn't.

"Surprise," she whispered again.

His groan was so loud he was afraid his parents would hear.

His parents? Hell, the whole neighborhood might have heard it through his open window.

Alex stared down into her dark, fathomless eyes, his blood thundering through his veins at a record pace. Despite the trashy trappings, he saw not the red wig or the offensive jewelry, but the woman beneath it all. The woman was a dazzling array of vivid puzzle pieces. The problem was that he couldn't seem to make them fit. And his frustration with failing had him tightly in its grip.

Nicole tunneled her hand inside the front of his slacks and grasped his throbbing arousal, making him grit his teeth.

"Come on, Alex," she whispered into his ear then nipped his lobe, causing him to shudder. "Tell me about the fantasies you had when you were a teenager in this bed. Have you ever had a girl up here? Did you ever get caught doing things you shouldn't have been doing?"

Her suggestive words further stoked the flames burning out of control in Alex's groin. He possessively grabbed the bare, swollen flesh between her legs. She gasped and softly cried out, "Yes."

Alex took in her flushed face, eyeing the way she repeatedly licked her lips, and he bucked when she ground against him.

"No," he growled.

He rolled to stand next to the bed, staring down at her longingly, wanting to take her and take her again, but knowing he shouldn't. The sound of something dropping came from the direction of the hall. No doubt his mother and sister had their ears pressed against the door, listening. He refused to give them anything else to hear.

Capturing Nicole's unfocused gaze, he pointed a finger at her, then jabbed a thumb into his chest. "You and me, we need to talk. Later. At the loft." Then he turned to the door. "And take off that damn wig and ridiculous jewelry."

DINNER WAS A TRIAL in patience at best, a complete fiasco at worst. Oh, everything looked the same, with the added exception of their unexpected guest. His mother put the roast simmered in red sauce along with *manestra*—a ricelike Greek pasta—on the table. There was also salad, *tiropitas*—cheese pastries—and a plate of broiled sausages and broccoli. Red retsina wine was poured into stubby glasses and bread was passed around.

And with every breath Nicole went out of her way to say the wrong thing, move the wrong way and generally make Alex's blood pressure rise higher and higher.

At first his mother hadn't known what to do with her, but as the meal went on she seemed to look at Nicole in a way that spoke of understanding and maybe even a bit of baffled affection. During the course of the dinner, even his father seemed to laugh at Nicole's jokes instead of at her. And Athena...Athena had shocked the hell out of him by joining in the outrageous behavior, the two women seeming to bond on a level he couldn't hope to understand.

Three hours later he slammed the door to the loft, watching Nicole walk blissfully into the apartment in front of him. Early evening sunlight slanted through the windows, filling the dark room with an orange-yellow glow.

"Where's the jewelry, Nicole?" he said evenly, trying to move beyond her offensive display at his parents' house and return to a neutral topic so he might regain his temper.

She leaned a hand against one of the black steel support columns and reached to slip off her shoes. Damn it all, but it was all he could do not to tell her to leave them on.

"You asked me to take it off, remember?" At least she had done that much, but she had kept on that seductive wig. "It's in my purse."

What she carried wasn't a purse, it was a suitcase. A backpack designed to hold everything she needed so she could bolt at the drop of a hat.

And, unfortunately, Alex was this close to dropping that hat.

He was...humiliated. Ashamed. And pissed as all get out that she'd done what she had. As the oldest, he'd always strived to make his parents proud of him. Especially after he moved to Manhattan and refused to go into business with his father. Yes, he'd taken both his previous girlfriends home for an occasional dinner. But they had dressed the part and had been courteous and respectful to his parents.

Nicole had seemed to take everything his parents believed in, crushed it into a ball and thrown it back into their faces.

"I'm going to take a shower," she said with a smile. "Wanna join me?"

Alex was too afraid he'd drown her under the penetrating spray even as he slammed his body into hers.

"You're still upset."

He threw his keys to the counter then put down the bag of leftovers his mother had sent home with him, just like she sent home every Sunday. "Upset doesn't begin to cover it, Nic. Take your damn shower. Hopefully by the time you come out I'll be calm enough to talk without wanting to kill you."

A shadow entered her eyes but she wisely chose not to say anything as she grabbed her backpack then disappeared into the bathroom.

Alex crossed to his bed. It was left unmade and he could swear he still smelled the evidence of the sex Nicole and he had had that morning. He turned and sank down into the mattress, rubbing the heels of his hands against his closed eyelids.

Christ, what was he going to do? Not just about what happened today and the inevitable questions his parents would ask him about the strumpet he'd brought home to dinner. But about the entire situation, period. Had he known there was even a chance this would have happened, he never would have pulled Nicole in on this case. Essentially she'd undone what had taken him thirty-two years to do. In one afternoon she had stripped away his good son persona and made him look like a lust-crazed fool in front of his family.

He pulled in a deep breath then let it out in a long sigh.

"Damn."

He'd forgotten Athena had wanted to talk to him. Just another reason why he should be upset with the woman in the other room.

He sat there for so long trying to make sense out of her and the inexplicable things she did to him he didn't notice her come out of the bathroom until she stood in front of him.

His jaw tightened as he lifted his head and stared at her bare, moisture-covered body, wearing nothing but the Tiffany jewelry she'd lifted the other day and a decadent smile.

He sat paralyzed, shocked and angry and wanting more than anything to push her away.

"You're still mad."

He glared at her.

She stepped closer, moving her legs to either side of his so that her smooth vulva slit open invitingly.

No...he wasn't going to give in to his lust for her again. He needed her out of his life. Now. Tonight.

She pushed at his shoulders, causing her breasts to sway in front of him.

"Shh. Don't say a word. You're so tense." She began unbuttoning his shirt. "And I know just the thing to relax you...."

Alex wanted to grab her arms and shake her. Rip the stolen jewels, the evidence of her illegal activities, from around her beautiful neck.

He wanted to slam into her like there was no tomorrow.

A low sound of frustration and anger and need swirled up from his chest and exited his mouth in a low roar as he grabbed her and pushed her into the mattress. "Do you have any idea what you're doing to me? Any idea at all?"

She gave him a naughty, knowing smile as she flattened her hands against his chest, then slid them down to where he was rock-hard. "Mmm. I think I have an idea."

Before he could take a breath, she was cradling him in her damp fingers. He closed his eyes and swallowed hard, the red-hot sensations collecting inside him nearing the boiling point.

She ripped open his shirt and pressed her wet breasts against his bare chest, multiplying his heartbeat by two.

She pushed his legs open where he hovered over her then slid down, leaving him supporting his weight against his hands. He heard his zipper slide down then felt her hot, hot mouth taking him in inch by shuddering inch.

Dear God...

Alex caught the rumpled top sheet in his fists and strained against orgasm. She licked and squeezed and sucked until his blood roared past his ears, until his breathing was little more than ragged gasps, and until he was a blink away from coming.

Then she released him.

She slid back up until her head was even with his again then laced her arms around his neck and kissed him. He felt her breath against his ear. "Tell me what I do to you, Alex."

At this point he was beyond words. He was too busy shaking out of his pants. "Shut up and give me a rubber."

She reached up and produced a packet from under one of the bed pillows, her smile pure sin as she handed it to him.

"Put it on," he ordered.

He felt her shiver, her reaction to his domineering demeanor turning him on even further.

Nicole spread her legs wider and ran the unsheathed length of him through her hot dripping channel. Dear God, but Alex wanted more than anything to pump into her wicked flesh, pregnancy and STDs be damned.

He wanted to feel her. All of her. Pure, burning and unfettered.

Sandwiching him between her swollen folds, she began rolling down the condom, taking her time about it all, a teasing gleam in her eyes that told him she knew what she was doing.

A gleam that left when he savagely thrust into her to the hilt.

Nicole's eyelids fluttered closed and she arched her neck, a low, almost silent moan escaping her mouth. He thrust again. And again. His movements wild. Utterly selfish. Totally greedy.

Her flesh clenched around him and shudders racked her frame. She was climaxing. The quickness amazed him. And sent him hurtling over the edge right along with her.

9

SOMEWHERE AROUND MIDNIGHT Nicole lay with her head at the foot of the bed, her feet resting against the iron headboard while Alex was stretched at the right angle, his feet next to her head.

When they'd returned from his parents' earlier, she'd thought for sure he was going to ask her to leave. Pack up her things and take a hike. Which wouldn't have been too difficult because everything she owned she either wore or had in her backpack. The prospect of his actions disturbed her in a way she wasn't equipped to deal with. When relationships went bad, she was usually the first one out the door, no questions, no recriminations, no drawn-out goodbyes.

But the thought of never seeing Alex again...

She felt a chill even though the night was warm and the fan rattling nearby did little more than regurgitate the warm air.

What she did know was that she wanted to stay until whatever was happening between them played out to its natural conclusion. So she'd taken a shower and formulated a plan to seduce him, all the while afraid it was too late. That she had gone too far.

She turned her head to stare out the window at the dark night beyond. She wasn't really sure why she'd done what she had today. She'd merely wanted to make a point of sorts. Only the point itself was a little blurry.

Had she been trying to prove to him that no one controlled her? Or had she been paying him back for having followed her to Nessbaum's? For making her feel guilty about doing something she did every day of the week without an ounce of remorse? Or had a small part of her been trying to force him to end whatever was happening between them because she was incapable of walking away?

She felt oddly...sad at the possibility. It didn't help that her entire body throbbed and ached. She'd thought everything would be okay if she could entice him into sex. But the end result was far from okay. While a part of her was strangely glad that he couldn't resist her, another questioned the roughness of his lovemaking. He'd slammed into her again and again with little shame, taking her breath away. He'd stroked her breasts roughly, his movements speaking of his need for possession and absolute submission to his needs. And she'd given him everything he demanded. Hoping in some kind of twisted way that the answers she sought lay in this new dimension to their relationship.

Instead she now felt oddly...empty. As if what she'd done and his resulting actions, had destroyed whatever tentative bonds had been developing between them.

Only she didn't know what those bonds were and what they meant. She did know that this morning she'd felt a slight panic at his leaving her to go to his parents' for dinner. Not because he hadn't invited her. They'd only known each other a few days so she could understand that. Rather she'd felt almost...scared, somehow. As if his contact with his normal life, his family, would spotlight all her faults and failings and he would return to the loft and find her lacking.

So what did she do? She'd acted on that fear. Not in a positive way. Rather she'd basically guaranteed that what she'd feared would happen, *did* happen. A sort of self-fulfilling prophecy.

Emotion clogged her throat, momentarily choking off air.

She was startled when Alex reached out and rested his hand against her thigh. She'd thought he was asleep.

The light touch was reassuring somehow, though he said nothing.

Nicole stared at the Tiffany jewelry she'd taken off earlier and put on the bedside table. It looked surreal in the dim light from the full moon filtering in through the window. "My mom had this really pretty brooch," she whispered, her voice raspy from having cried out so often during the past few hours. "She didn't have much jewelry. She wasn't a jewelry-type person, you know?"

She paused, trying to judge if Alex was listening. He didn't move or say anything.

"The brooch was a gift from my dad on their wedding day." She turned her head toward him. "Not stolen. They spent their wedding night at the Waldorf Astoria and went on a few long strolls through the city." She smiled sadly, hating that she had to qualify everything. "One of their walks took them past Tiffany's."

It had been a long time since she'd thought of her mother. Remembered what life had been like with her in it. Yet during the past few days with Alex, she'd found herself dusting out that corner of her mind, tentatively exploring it.

But he appeared to have completely closed himself off to her.

She tried to move her leg away from his touch, her emotional condition too raw, the memories of her mother telling her this story too vivid. "I don't know why I'm telling you this. You don't want to hear it."

Alex refused to release his grip. But where his touch had been possessively rough earlier, now it was unbearably gentle.

"What happened to the brooch?" he asked.

Nicole blinked to stare at the ceiling, trying to dry the tears that had accumulated in the corners of her eyes. "I don't know. I think my father may have buried it with her." She paused. "Oh, how she loved that brooch." She closed her eyes. "She used to get it out every Sunday and wear it to dinner. She never wore it outside. She joked that she and Dad never went anywhere for her to wear it anyway. And even if they had, she would be too afraid to wear it outside, you know, in case someone would steal it."

Silence stretched between them. Nicole swore she could hear her own heart beating and was convinced that if she listened hard enough, she might hear Alex's, too.

"Did she approve of your father's profession?"

She took in his words and moved them around her mind. "What? Plumbing?"

She heard him move. She looked to find him studying her.

She smiled as she said softly, "My mother never knew what my father did before she met him."

"But when she died..."

She cleared her throat. "When she died, he hung up his tool belt for good and returned to being a full-time thief."

"And brought you into the business with him."

Her heartbeat leapt. "No. My brother and I...we'd been getting into a lot of trouble at school. You know, playing hooky, fighting with other kids, insulting teachers. My father didn't know what to do with me and Jeremy. So he started teaching us how to plumb."

She saw Alex smile in the dark.

Nicole smiled back. "Don't laugh. I could repipe this entire building."

She turned her face away, the sadness within her spreading instead of lessening. She thought of the past, of her mother, her father, her brother and what had happened to them all. She'd never pitied herself before. Had never given herself permission to grieve what could have been. She'd merely forged ahead and survived the best way she knew how.

Her gaze rested on the jewelry again. "You know, I never keep the Tiffany pieces I steal permanently," she whispered. "I only keep them for a couple of days then I make sure they get back to their rightful owner. Anonymously, of course."

Silence, then a quiet, "I know."

The empty space in her chest filled briefly with warmth. She'd never really experienced the power of a shared knowing before. Understanding. Acceptance that what she said was true.

Nicole heard Alex shift. When she turned her head

to see what he was doing, she found him hovering over her. He nudged her knees apart and stared intensely down into her eyes. She didn't sense any anger in him. No need to possess her. Instead the man looking at her ranged somewhere between the angry Alex and the uptight yet adventurous guy she'd first met.

"Tell me why you did that today," he said quietly.

She tried to turn her head away. He caught her chin in his fingers and gently turned her back to meet his gaze. "Tell me."

She looked at his wide chest and shoulders through her lashes, thinking that maybe she should try to break her habit of seeking out guys with those qualities. But even as she thought it, she knew that she wouldn't be seeking out any man other than Alex for a long time to come. "I was scared."

His breathing was even, patient. "Scared of what?"

She blinked to look into his eyes. "Scared of losing you." She swallowed hard. "Scared of not losing you."

He squinted at her, as if trying to make sense out of her words.

"Don't try," she told him. "I don't understand it either."

He gave her a soft, crooked smile. "Oh, I think I understand more than you know, Nic."

Then he dipped his head to kiss her.

Nicole's breath caught. She was still as he brushed his lips against hers, then kissed the right corner of her mouth...then the left. The warmth in her chest expanded outward, making her shiver again, but this time for a different reason. This time because she felt cherished instead of used.

Alex pulled back slightly, smoothing her hair back from her face. "So beautiful..."

Nicole wanted to look away, but couldn't. She read in his eyes, his expression, his touch, complete sincerity. And the honesty almost proved too much for her to bear.

"When I first saw you in Baltimore, I thought that my grandmother would say you had the eyes of a witch." He gently kissed her right brow. "The kind of eyes that could make men do things they otherwise wouldn't." He lowered his mouth to press his lips against her closed eyelid then moved to her other eye. "I wish my grandmother could have met you."

Nicole's heart skipped a beat. That he should be so generous after what she'd done to his parents made her heart ache.

"She would have given you as much hell as you'd have given her," he murmured, lowering his mouth until he nuzzled her chin. "Unfortunately it's that fire, that spunk, that got her killed."

Such serious words said in such a soft way made Nicole stiffen.

"It's okay. It was a long time ago. She was working at my father's grocery. One afternoon while she was working by herself a couple of thugs came in and started lifting the more expensive items. Instead of raising the alarm, she went for the shotgun behind the counter. Only the thieves got off a round first."

Nicole gently grasped his head in her hands. "Oh, Alex. I'm sorry."

He paused and laid his head between her breasts. "That's the reason I decided to become a cop, you know? I always thought that one day I'd catch up with the guys who killed *Yiayia*, my grandmother."

Nicole ran her fingers slowly, lightly over his silky hair.

She was surprised when she felt his tongue against her breast. "You do something to me, Nicole." He lifted his head to look at her. "I don't know what it is, or how you do it, but I'm not the same guy I was before I met you." He smiled. "Maybe my grandmother would have been right. You bewitched me from the first moment I looked into those magnificent eyes of yours."

She quietly laughed, but there was little humor there.

"All I know is that I can't seem to get enough of you."

The words were said so quietly that Nicole almost didn't hear them. But more important than the words was the intense emotion that lurked behind them.

"All I can think of is kissing you," he murmured, his fingers finding and encircling her right breast. "Of running my tongue over your body." He squeezed the soft flesh then took her nipple into his mouth, sucking lightly.

Her heart beat a hammering rhythm in her chest.

"Of touching you…"

He slid his hand down to her rib cage, then over her waist, his thumb pausing at her navel before drifting down lower to her vulva.

Her breath caught as he used his index finger and thumb to part her swollen folds. Tender flesh that burned and ached from the angry sex they'd had earlier. He slid down and blew on the delicate area. "Of tasting you..."

He moved the tip of his tongue around her tight bud, then pulled the button of flesh between his lips, nibbling before he sucked.

Nicole's back came up off the mattress as flames licked over her skin, setting her on fire.

"So soft," he whispered, running his thumbs over her cleanly shaven labia. "So sweet."

He took her into his mouth again and she moaned, grabbing handfuls of bed linens in her fists.

She watched through her lashes, transfixed, as he slowly slid two fingers up into her body then twisted them clockwise, providing a sensation she'd never experienced before. He withdrew his fingers then slowly entered her again, this time turning them counterclockwise, then following the curve of the vaginal walls, slightly curling his fingers until he hit her G-spot. He gently rubbed the nerve center then increased the suction of his mouth, sending Nicole soaring into a world of white-hot sensation.

She slowly glided back to earth, her breathing ragged, her skin covered in sweat. She looked down to find Alex's head lying across her stomach. She moved to smooth back his hair, finding her hand trembling from the intensity of her orgasm.

"Good?" he whispered.

She smiled languidly. "Good doesn't begin to cover it."

He lifted himself to a sitting position, then brought her up to straddle his hips. She wrapped her legs and arms around him, holding tight to everything that was him. Everything solid and safe and so very sexy.

She clung to him for a long moment, feeling his heart beat against hers. She felt like she'd been given a rare second chance. She stared into his eyes while he unwrapped a condom and sheathed himself. Then, finally, he was filling her. Entirely. Completely. Slowly.

The word slowly caught in her mind, but she couldn't respond to it. Felt no need, no urgency to speed things up. Instead, she let him set the pace. Just like she had earlier in the day when he'd seemed intent on punishing her for her bad judgment.

The emotions rolling through her were terrifying...yet oddly freeing. And she was helpless to do anything but give herself over to them.

Alex smoothed his hands over Nicole's hips then inched them back to her bottom, parting her slightly to allow for deeper penetration. He stretched his neck back and gritted his teeth as she took every millimeter of him deep into her body, her heat completely engulfing him.

He couldn't pinpoint the exact moment Nicole had surrendered to him. Earlier, she'd given as good as she got, meeting his almost violent attention with an aggression of her own. Now...

He gently lifted her hips then slowly brought her back down again.

Now she seemed content to trust him.

He stroked her supple bottom, sensing they had reached a turning point, moved beyond the fork they had faced a little while ago.

Sweat dripped from his forehead, sloping down his nose then dropping to where her breasts swayed against his chest. He'd been so very close to shutting her out of his life for good. And now it seemed there wasn't a person in this world that he felt closer to.

He slid his hands up her silken back then buried his fingers in her long, dark hair. She hummed and bent her head back. The look of pure passion on her face made his heart pump all the harder.

In and out...in and out. Their bodies moved as if in slow motion, prolonging the strokes, exploring sensations neither had experienced before.

And when they reached climax, they did so together, their bodies intertwined, the connection complete....

"A PERSON COULD get used to this."

"Mmm," Alex agreed.

He rubbed the arch of his foot against the top of Nicole's under the breakfast bar in his kitchen. Neither of them wore anything but smiles where they sat on the chrome-and-red vinyl stools. The Monday morning sun was just beginning to break the horizon outside the windows. The fan rattled and spit, but otherwise the world was silent and dark and intimate as he and Nicole sat drinking much-needed coffee.

"Are you sure you have to go into work this morning?" she murmured, tucking her glorious dark hair behind her ear.

Cat jumped up onto the counter to see what the fuss was about. Alex didn't even flinch, not caring where the fearless feline went at this point. He was coming to see the truth in the saying that you didn't own a cat; rather, they owned you.

Cat sniffed his coffee cup, narrowed his eyes at him, then butted his head against his hand. Alex lethargically scratched him behind the ears. "Sorry, dude, but that's all the energy I can spare right now."

Cat twitched his tail then jumped off the counter and sashayed back to his favorite chair in the corner.

Nicole smiled. "If I didn't know better, I'd say you two have called a truce."

Alex wanted to say that they weren't the only ones. Wanted to tell Nicole that his head had called a truce in the battle with his heart. It didn't matter what she did or didn't do for a living. He loved her.

The words should have caught him by surprise. But they didn't. Now that he'd identified the feeling that had taken him by storm, he recognized he'd had all the warning signs.

"What are you grinning about?" Nicole whispered, upping the ante in their game of footsie by walking her toes up the inside of his leg.

"I'm not grinning."

She laughed as she put her cup down. "You are, too."

He considered her in the dim purple light of dawn. He felt his face. "Oh, yeah. I guess I am."

Nicole's other foot followed the same path as the first until she had both feet in his lap. She gazed at him as she took a long sip of coffee. "Do you really have to go into work this morning?"

"Mmm." Alex took a *koulouraki*—a Greek vanilla cookie—from the plate his mother had sent home with him then pushed the rest toward Nicole. "Someone has to keep this boat afloat."

She snickered as she bit into a cookie. "Boat afloat, huh?"

He nodded, chasing his own cookie with coffee.

She considered him. "You're going ahead with that fake policy, aren't you?" she asked quietly.

He didn't say anything.

"You know the auction is tomorrow, don't you? And that the most likely time for D.M. to hit it will be tonight when the staff are readying the pieces for display."

"Yes." He avoided her gaze. "And I don't want you anywhere near that place."

"I thought you didn't think it was D.M.'s target."

"I don't."

"Well, that makes a lot of sense."

"It does, doesn't it?" He grinned, blithely ignoring her sarcasm. "Anyway, I hope to have this thing wrapped up tonight, so there won't be any reason for you to go to that auction."

She was shaking her head. "I can't believe how off base you are."

He wasn't willing to discuss that just now. He was enjoying the no-conflict zone they were currently in the middle of and didn't want to upset it.

"By the way, my sister wouldn't happen to have let on what she wanted to talk to me about while you two were doing dishes yesterday, did she?"

Nicole's chewing slowed, as if the mention of what had happened at his parents' upset her.

"Never mind. I'll give her a call today." He dipped another cookie into his cup. "After meeting you, I wonder if she's decided to bring her own boyfriend home."

"Boyfriend?"

Alex nodded. "I figure that's got to be the reason she stays away from home so often."

Nicole stared at her cup. "I suppose that's one way of looking at it."

"And another way would be?"

She looked up. "That Athena may be bringing her girlfriend home."

He shrugged. "No big deal. My parents have already met all of her..."

He drifted off as he realized that by "girlfriend" Nicole didn't mean old buddy, old pal, but rather...

"Lover?" he nearly croaked.

Nicole smiled and nodded.

"She told you that?"

"You didn't know?"

"No, I didn't know. Isn't that obvious?" He thrust his fingers into his hair and held them there. "Holy shit, my mother's going to have a cow."

"I think your mother's made of sterner stuff than you give her credit for." She shrugged as she reached for his cup then dipped her cookie into his coffee. She bit into it. "Besides, homosexuality wasn't exactly invented yesterday, you know. From what I understand, the Greeks have been onto it for years. Centuries even."

Alex stared at her. "Very funny."

"I thought you needed a reality check."

He grumbled under his breath and gently moved her feet from his lap so he could get up. "I'd better go catch a shower and get ready for work."

"Care for some company?"

He grinned at her. "Oh, I think I can come up with a thing or two you can wash for me...."

IT HAD BEEN A WHILE since Nicole had been behind the wheel of a car. It had taken her a good five minutes to grow accustomed to the sensitivity of the brakes and accelerator of the used compact she had rented downtown. She fussed with the visor so she could block the late-morning summer sun streaming in through the windows, then cranked up the air conditioner. The car next to her beeped. Oops. She'd drifted into the other lane.

She righted the car then waved her apologies to the other driver.

Who needed a cell phone to get into an accident? Native New Yorkers who weren't used to driving were a danger unto themselves.

She glanced at the dash clock, trying to estimate the time she'd be back in the city. It all depended on how long her visit took. She shivered then reached to turn the temperature back up again, not sure if her nervousness or the car's internal cooling system was to blame for her heat flashes.

She thought of Alex and smiled softly.

Last night...

Another beep.

She righted the car again and decided that if she hoped to stay alive, last night should remain right where it was. For now.

Her turnoff was coming up and she was way in the wrong lane. She flicked on the blinker and edged a path over two lanes before sloping down the off-ramp. Her palms were sweaty as hell, which could be a result of the hairy driving experience or of what lay ahead. She wiped them one at a time against her simple black cotton dress then took a deep breath.

An hour and this will be over with, she repeated like a

drowning man clinging to a buoy and hoping the coast guard would happen by.

Fifteen minutes later she had parked, squeaked through the thorough security and was sitting at a metal table with bolted down chairs in the meeting area of Shawongunk Correctional Facility in Wallkill, New York, waiting for her father to be led in.

"What am I doing here?" she whispered, staring at the armed guards at either door to the room, another pair of visitors to her right. Merely being in the place made her skin itch and coated her stomach with mercury.

"Hi."

Nicole hadn't realized her father had been brought in until he stood before her, grinning like she'd just done something monumentally important like taken home the Nobel Peace Prize. Of course, she didn't think the committee had a prize named for thievery.

"Hi, yourself," she whispered, awkwardly hugging him.

In the worn denim shirt and blue work pants her father looked closer to the plumber she remembered rather than an accomplished thief. She couldn't help thinking that if he had remained a plumber, he wouldn't be sitting in prison.

Still, love filled her to overflowing for the man who had raised her and her brother as best as he could. He'd quietly dealt with his own pain after his wife had died and instead dealt with the pain of their children, a son and daughter who were by his side, witnessing their mother's slow death and now only had him to rely on. And in the months, then years, following that awful day, he'd never taken his frustration out on them.

She smiled softly. And there certainly had never been a dull moment.

Her father took a seat across from her and rested his hands on the table. "I'm surprised to see you. Surprised, but glad."

Nicole stared at her own hands, guilt melding with her discomfort at being inside the drab prison even if it was only for a visit. "I would have come earlier, but..."

But what? She hadn't been able to bolster the courage to see her father sitting behind bars for a crime he'd committed? Hadn't been able to handle visiting a place that she could very well end up in herself one day?

Her father touched her hands. "Hey, it's okay."

Nicole slid her hands out of reach. "No, Dad, it's not okay." She sat back and crossed her arms over her chest to ward off a chill as much as to prevent him from touching her in a way that reminded her too much of the father she'd once known. "I hate seeing you in this place. I hate seeing you wearing...that." She shuddered. "I wish..."

She fell silent.

At the far corner of the room metal clanked and she could just make out the quiet conversation of the couple nearby.

She wished what? That her mother had never died? That he had never hung up his plumber's belt and that even now she was lying under someone's sink repairing a clogged drain?

She absently rubbed her forehead. This was so not like her. She'd never had much time for what if's and what could have been's. She'd always been firmly planted in reality.

"I wish things could have worked out differently," she finally finished her sentence.

"So do I."

She looked at him, all too aware that they weren't talking about the same thing. More than likely he was wishing that his lawyer had been able to plea bargain a better deal or had been able to find a technicality to get him off on.

"Hey, why the long face, Hal?" Her father used the shortened version of her real name then chuckled in that way that had always made her feel like everything was going to be all right. "We all know the nature of this business. What's the first thing I taught you and Jeremy when you both decided to follow in your old man's footsteps?"

She sighed, thinking about how long ago that had been. "You get caught doing the crime, you do the time."

"That's right." He folded his hands. "Besides, all told even this detour makes it worth it, you know? I mean even though I'm out of commission, I'll make more per annum than I ever would have as a plumber."

Nicole rolled her eyes and laughed. "Trust you to find a silver lining."

He shrugged.

She cleared her throat. "The problem is I'm having a little more trouble finding any precious metal these days."

He squinted at her for a long time. "This, my being sent up, really got to you, didn't it?"

"That and a few other things."

"Ah. You've met someone."

Nicole's gaze snapped to his face.

"What, you seem surprised."

She folded her own hands on the table. "Maybe it's because I am."

He pointed a finger at her. "The expression you're wearing? That's the way I looked when I met your mom."

Nicole's throat felt suddenly thick.

He sighed in memory. "Oh, there wasn't anything I wouldn't have done for your mom, Hal. There was this special something about her, you know? The moment she asked me to stop, I knew I would."

Nicole blinked. "What? Mom knew?"

He grinned. "Your mom knew everything. Even if I hadn't told her, she would have figured it out." He seemed to be looking through Nicole rather than at her. "I remember the first time I tried to give her a piece of stolen jewelry. It was a beautiful necklace. Sapphires that exactly matched the color of her eyes." He seemed to focus on his daughter now. "She made me take it back to where I got it and promise that I would never do anything like that again. And I didn't. At least not until—"

"Not until she died," Nicole whispered.

Her mother had known. The information made her head spin. She'd always assumed that her mother had never known what her father had done before meeting her, that her knowing would have ruined their relationship. Had her mother seen something in her father that went beyond his illegal activities? Or had it been love that had made her believe he was redeemable?

A guard walked by their table. "Five minutes."

Her father nodded, his expression growing more intense as he looked at Nicole. "I'm sorry this had to happen, Hal. And I'm sorry you're having such a hard time with it." He ran his hands over his thick, graying hair several times. "Had I known I was being set up..."

Nicole felt the air rush from her lungs. "Dad? Do you know the name of the man who set you up? D.M.?"

He nodded. "Of course. I don't work with anyone I don't know." He frowned. "I only wished I had known him a little better." He rattled off a name.

For the past six days she and Alex had been trying to uncover D.M.'s identity. And here her father had just handed it to her during casual conversation.

She got up from the chair then curved her arms around his neck and gave him a loud kiss on the cheek. "Thank you, Dad."

She tried to draw away, but he held her close. "God, Hal, do you know how much it hurts me to see you hurting?" His breath stirred her hair. "I love you, you know? You and your brother." He pulled back slightly to smile into her face, his eyes damp. "You remember that, you hear? Always."

Nicole smiled back. She'd always known and she always would.

10

WHERE WAS SHE?

Alex stepped past his secretary without acknowledging her, then stopped himself with a hand on the doorjamb of his office. "Any calls?" he asked.

Dorothy blinked at him. "Yes. I just told you there were three—"

Alex was at her desk before she could finish and took the three message slips from her hand. His superior wanting a status report. A return call from the private detective agency saying nothing had moved on the stakeout of the faux policy. The third from his sister that just said she'd try again.

Nothing from Nicole.

He started back to his office, then remembered to thank Dorothy.

"You're welcome," she said as he closed the door.

He shrugged out of his jacket and hung it on the back of his chair before sitting down. At lunchtime he'd gone by the loft with takeout Chinese to see if she wanted to find inventive things to do with the chopsticks, only to find her gone. Cat hadn't even been there, but, then again, that wasn't saying too much because the open window allowed the fearless feline to come and go as he pleased via the fire escape.

When Alex had finally left Nicole this morning she'd been smiling, happily stretched out between his sheets.

He'd fully expected to find her still there, catching up on much-needed sleep. But the bed had been made, the loft cleaned up and she had been long gone.

Okay, so Nicole wasn't the type to account for her whereabouts to anybody. But with everything coming to a head in the investigation, and given where things stood between them on a more personal front, he at least thought she'd give him a call, let him know what she was up to, what she had in mind.

The phone rang at his elbow. He snatched it up on the first ring.

"Cassavetes," he barked.

"Alex?"

Not Nicole. He grimaced. And not only was it not Nicole, it was his mother.

He switched the receiver to his other ear and reached for the D.M. file. "Did you expect Dad to be at the number you dialed, Ma?"

He expected a laugh. Instead he got silence.

"What is it?" he asked grudgingly. Whenever his mom was serious, something was wrong. "Is it Athena again? Don't tell me. She didn't come home last night."

"No, no. I mean, yes, she didn't come home again last night, but that's not why I'm calling."

Alex waited for her to continue.

Then it hit him. The reason she was calling.

Nicole.

Damn.

He really wasn't up for this conversation right now. Not when his own emotions were still up in the air concerning the sexy, reckless brunette. "Mom, I can explain..."

He could? This, he'd like to hear.

Only he didn't get a chance to say anything, because his mother beat him to the punch.

"Alex, my dowry is missing."

His brows shot up high on his forehead.

Okay, that hadn't been what he'd expected at all.

Nor was the pain in his solar plexus as if someone had just hit him square with a sucker punch.

His mother's dowry, as she called it, was a set of antique black pearl jewelry that had been a gift from her mother, and her grandmother before that. In Greece, dowries were still expected when a daughter married. But in his mother's case, the only items of worth his grandparents had owned had been the jewelry set. And it had been worth far more than anyone would have believed. After coming to New York, his mother had taken it in to sell to pay a portion of the rent they were behind. But the appraisal had been so high, she'd insured the jewelry instead and used it as collateral for a loan. A loan large enough to pay the rent, lease shop space and give the Cassavetes the financial boost they'd needed.

And now the jewelry was missing.

"What do you mean it's missing?" he asked, telling himself this couldn't be happening. That his mother had to have moved it and forgotten where she had moved it to.

"I mean it's gone, Alexanthros. What else does 'missing' mean?"

A dull ache started at his temples. His parents should have listened to him when he told them they should put the pieces in a safety deposit box at their bank. But no, his mother hadn't trusted the bank. Besides, she'd argued, what point was there in having something if you didn't have it?

"Have you talked to Dad?"

"Of course I talked to your father. He wants to call the police."

"Is there anything else missing?" Alex asked, going into professional mode and trying to forget that he was talking to his mother, and that the pieces meant so much to his family.

"No."

"When's the last time you saw the pieces?"

"Two days ago."

With each response, Alex's heart dropped lower and lower in his chest.

"You don't suppose..." his mother said. "I mean, you don't think..." Alex closed his eyes. "That girl you brought over...she was a bit on the strange side, don't you think? You don't suppose..."

Alex pushed his chair back and stood up. "I've got to go, Ma. I'll...I'll call you later, okay?"

"Should I call the police, like your father wants?"

"No," he said. "Not yet."

"Okay. Okay."

He began to say goodbye.

"You know how very much that jewelry means to me, Alexandros? Means to this family? I planned to give it to your sister on her wedding day...."

"I know, Ma. I know."

Minutes later, Alex slowly replaced the receiver sure of two things: Nicole had taken his mother's jewelry, and he would never forgive her for it.

NICOLE LET HERSELF into the loft, dropped her backpack to the floor then carried the bags of groceries she'd bought into the kitchen area. Cat wiggled through the narrow window opening and hurried across the loft to her, silently pounding on the black wood floor. The cat leapt onto the counter and meowed loudly, either welcoming Nicole back, or complaining that she'd been gone too long. Nicole chose to believe the former.

"Were you watching for me, C?" she asked, putting the bags down then scratching the temperamental tom behind the ears. "You were, weren't you, you little devil you?"

She began lining up the items from the bags, smiling as she did so.

The visit with her father had given her plenty to mull over during the ninety-minute drive back into the city. With each mile that had disappeared under the tires, her uneasiness had dissipated. Not because she was no longer within the prison walls, but because she had visited her dad there.

Her father didn't make any excuses. He never had. She suspected she'd gone in projecting her own growing fear of incarceration onto him, expecting to find him broken, repentant or, like so many others she knew, a bible-thumping born-again Christian damning his prior sins. But she had found only him, the same man she had known all of her life. The grinning, shrugging, easygoing man who had helped shape her into the independent, strong woman she was today.

He was also the man who had just set her free. The man who had shared the story of his past and offered promising possibility for Nicole's future.

She tucked her hair behind her ear. Fear had fueled

what she'd done at Alex's parents' yesterday. But she now knew that fear itself had been fueled by concern that their relationship could never go further than it already had.

She made a face. Why did life always have to be so complicated?

Of course, she'd never really realized how complicated it could be until she'd met Alex. Only she would fall in love with the one man opposite from her in so many ways. She was a thief; he was an ex-cop/insurance investigator. She prided herself on being original; he was as conventional as they came.

And he had touched her heart in a way no other man before him had ever come close to doing.

Cat meowed, watching her with first curiosity, then growing wariness.

"What? You don't trust me to cook?"

Cat plopped his butt down on the counter and narrowed his eyes at her.

If Nicole didn't know better, she'd think he remembered the last time she'd tried her hand at cooking. It had been last Easter, Jeremy and Joanna had just had Justine, and her father had yet to be sentenced. For some godforsaken reason, she'd decided to do dinner. What she'd ended up with even Cat had refused to touch.

"I'm doing something simple this time. See?" she asked, showing the hypercritical feline the package of fresh pasta. "Spaghetti with garlic bread. Even I can handle that."

Cat was doubtful.

Not that she blamed him. While she talked a good

game, she was scared to death that something would still go wrong.

She found herself rubbing the back of her neck, smoothing the small hairs there. All day she'd felt ill at ease. Initially she'd thought it was because of the anxiety surrounding her visit to her father. And now she considered that it might be worry that she would muck up even this simple dinner. But neither explanation seemed to do the trick.

Instead she had that eerie feeling that someone was following her again.

Ridiculous. The only one who had been looking for her had already found her.

Something seemed to tickle her from the inside out as her sigh filled the interior of the large loft. She switched on the portable radio behind her that was set to an oldies station, then searched the lower cupboards for the pans she would need.

For the next twenty minutes she worked steadily, putting a large pot of water on to boil for the pasta, then carefully chopping and measuring the ingredients she would need for the simple tomato sauce and putting them in a smaller pan. She turned around to check for salad fixings in the refrigerator and jumped.

"Alex!"

Standing off to the side of the kitchen, his arms crossed over his wide chest, Alex silently watched her.

Nicole's heart leapt in her chest and she began to smile.

Until she realized he wasn't smiling back.

HOURS LATER Alex sat on the empty, neatly made bed, his head heavy in his hands. Behind him the sun was setting through the windows, the only barometer of the passage of time. Strangely he felt caught in a time warp, his brain frozen, his body oddly incapable of movement. He felt as if he were trapped in a human-size trash compactor and the sides were pushing in on him. He wanted to swear, shout, hit something, but mostly he wanted to escape from the intense emotions roiling in him like building steam.

"I didn't take your mother's jewelry, Alex."

Nicole's recent words echoed through his mind again and again as did his refusal to believe her.

Then she'd left.

His numb brain seemed incapable of wrapping itself around that fact.

Oh, he remembered her gathering up Cat, picking up her backpack and walking out the door, murmuring an apology he couldn't decipher right now, but it was as if the information had yet to thoroughly sink through his shell-shocked state.

Was it possible to love someone you couldn't trust?

Outside the open window a horn honked and a native New Yorker shouted at another one, but it all seemed very far away somehow. As if he wasn't a part of the picture, but rather a preoccupied observer.

"I thought...well, it doesn't matter what I thought now, does it?" Nicole had said, her beautiful face drawn into long lines.

The problem was, it did matter.

If it were true, if she hadn't been the one behind the disappearance of his mother's jewelry, then she would have defended herself more, wouldn't she? Not just look at him with such an expression of guilt—or could it have been disappointment?—that his gut had wrenched.

Finally his muscles responded to a command. He pushed from the bed then turned to stare down at it. Flashes of the hours he and Nicole had spent right there whooshed through his mind.

He grabbed the pillows first, stripping off the cases that smelled like her fresh hair then tossing them to the floor. Next came the sheets. He ripped the top sheet off to the left, the bottom sheet to the right until he stared down at the naked mattress, the action seeming to spur the need for even greater action. He threw the bottom sheet down, and was about to follow with the top when he found himself instead drawing the stretch of cotton to his nose. He closed his eyes and breathed deeply. Nicole's unique musky scent filled his senses and filled him with a remorse so intense he wanted to shout out.

Damn it! Why couldn't he have chosen a nice girl to fall in love with? From the minute he'd knocked on her hotel room door in Baltimore, he'd known Nicole would be trouble. She inspired him to do things he would never even have thought of before. Her free, reckless spirit had sucked him in, making him crave something different, something wild. Made him want nobody but her.

He let the sheet drop from his hand, watching as it slowly drifted to cover the small pile of other linens at his feet.

The damnable thing about it was that he'd gone into all this with his eyes wide open. He'd known who she was. What she did for a living. He'd known that she breezed in and out of relationships with the staying power of an easterly wind. He'd known that her code of ethics was unlike anything he'd encountered before and, while they made a strange kind of sense, they were the polar opposite of his own beliefs. He'd known from the get-go that anything more than sex would be impossible for them.

Her stealing his mother's jewelry had been but a reminder.

He gathered up the sheets and carried them to the trash can where he stood stuffing them inside until only a corner hung out after he closed the lid.

But if he'd hoped the action would make him feel better, he was sadly mistaken.

The tick tock of his windup alarm clock on his bedside table penetrated his clouded mind and he slowly turned his head to look at it.

After eight.

The realization sunk in.

After eight.

Shit. He was supposed to meet the private detective he'd hired to stake out the Johnstone's at eight.

Feeling like a man emerging from a fire, he grabbed his jacket and rushed for the door. He could only hope the intangible burn scars wouldn't take too long to heal. And pray that one day the woman who had branded his heart with her dark and restless spirit would become nothing but a distant memory.

He pulled open the door to stare into the face of his sister Athena who had her hand up about to knock.

"Holy crap," she said, putting the same hand over her heart. "You scared me, Alex."

Alex could count the times his sister had come to the loft on one hand. Usually they met up at their parents' house and communicated via phone calls. That she was standing there now indicated the importance of her visit.

Remembering what Nicole had told him the night before made him take pause.

Athena smiled. "Got a minute, big brother?"

No, he really didn't, but he figured he should carve one out for her. "Let me just make a quick call." He strode toward the kitchen. "Come in."

He listened as she closed the door behind her while he punched in the numbers for the P.I.'s cell phone.

A couple of minutes later, after trying no fewer than three times and receiving nothing but ceaseless rings and voice mail, he dropped the receiver into its cradle and stood motionless.

"Problems?" Athena asked.

"Huh?" Alex turned to find her sitting on the chrome stool across the counter. The same stool Nicole had used only that morning.

He winced. Had it really been only a few hours ago that he and Nicole had sat right there in the warm pre-dawn glow talking like a couple of horny old married people?

"Are those sheets?"

Alex focused on his sister. She was staring at his garbage can. "What's on your mind, Athena?"

She blinked at him in mock innocence. "What, no coffee? Soda? Something to offer a guest you don't see every day?"

Alex opened the refrigerator then thudded down a can of beer. "Talk."

She made a face. "Gee, thanks, Alex. Mom would be proud."

Remembering his mother's call earlier, he winced. "Is this about Mom's jewelry?"

Athena took a sip of beer then grimaced. "You know about that already?"

He nodded. "Mom called me earlier."

"Mom?"

Alex ran his hand restlessly through his hair. "Look, Athena, if you're just going to repeat everything I say, then this really doesn't qualify as a conversation." He rested his hands against the countertop. "If this is about...well, you...um..."

Athena stared at him blankly.

"You know, the fact that you haven't brought a boyfriend home. Um, because, well, you don't have a boyfriend, you have a..."

Realization backlit her dark eyes. "You can't even say it, can you?"

He pushed from the counter. "Say what?"

"Homosexual. Lesbian. Either one would apply."

He grimaced. "Of course I can say the words. I'm just not used to saying them in connection to my own sister, that's all."

Athena ran her thumbnail the length of the beer can. "I know. Mom's going to have a cow when I tell her, isn't she?"

Recalling that's exactly the way he had described the situation, Alex opened the refrigerator and grabbed another can of beer. He cracked it open and took a long drag.

"Anyway, that's not what I'm doing here. I mean, it's good that you know and everything, but it's not like I've been keeping anything a secret. I just don't go around saying things like 'my lover says' or pretending that once the cat is finally out of the bag everything will be all right and Jane and I will be invited to Christmas dinner together." She shook her head. "I've pretty much accepted that isn't going to happen, so what's the rush?"

Alex's gaze was steady. "So what are you doing here?"

"To discuss the plans for Mom and Dad's thirty-fifth wedding anniversary party, of course." She pushed the beer away. "But I thought you knew that."

Alex wasn't getting it. "What does Mom and Dad's anniversary have to do with Mom's jewelry?"

Athena looked at him now as if he'd lost it. "Because I took it to have some of the loose strands repaired and have the set cleaned, that's why. You know, as part of their gift."

Alex's head spun and he had to grab onto the edge of the counter to keep from falling over.

"What?" he whispered. "You took the jewelry?"

"Of course I did, silly. Who did you think..." Her words drifted off but her expression made it clear that she knew exactly what he'd thought. So very wrongly thought.

He'd accused Nicole of a crime she didn't commit.

"Oh, no, Alex, you didn't?" Athena whispered. "You didn't think that Nic took the stuff, did you?"

His jaw was clenched so tightly he thought it might crack. "What in the hell was I supposed to think, Athena? Mom calls today frantic that her jewelry's been stolen. The last time she saw it was two days ago. And who was the only stranger in the house between then and now?"

Athena smacked her hand to her forehead. "Oh my

God, no." She stared at him. "You didn't outright accuse her of stealing the pieces, did you?"

His silence said more than he ever could at that moment.

"Jesus, Joseph and Mary, Alex! What were you thinking?"

She got up from the stool and began to pace back and forth across the loft.

Alex's voice was a fierce growl. "Why didn't you say something about this before?"

She stopped to stare at him. "Oh, no. Don't you even try to pin this on me, big brother. I've been trying to hook up with you for the past week to talk about this. It's you who's been too busy to talk. If you had slowed down to the speed limit, maybe none of this would have happened." She began pacing again, then stopped. "What would ever make you think Nicole would do something like that?"

Alex downed the rest of the beer he held then stared at the can, surprised he'd drunk the whole thing. "Stay out of this, Athena. There are things you don't know about."

She crossed her arms, looking as formidable as their mother ever could. "Try me."

He rounded the counter and faced off with her. "She's a damn professional thief, Athena."

Her eyes widened.

He nodded. "That's right. She steals for a living. And one of her favorite targets is jewelry." He didn't tell her that it was Tiffany jewelry because that would only serve to prove that she would never have targeted his mother's pieces anyway.

"I don't believe you," his sister said adamantly.

"Yeah, well, it doesn't matter what you believe because facts are facts."

She crossed the few feet separating them and poked her finger into his chest. "And the most important fact in this whole equation is that Nicole was the best damn thing that ever happened to you, Alex."

They stood staring at each other like that for long moments, neither of them blinking, backing down or adding anything.

Then finally Athena sighed. "I knew you were thick-headed, Alex, but I would never have guessed you were this stupid."

She picked up her purse from the counter and headed for the door.

Alex stood rooted to the spot for the second time that day, watching a woman walk away from him, powerless to stop her.

He couldn't be sure how long he'd stood there like that, staring at the empty space between him and the door, but finally his blood began flowing again. He grabbed the doorknob.

"Damn. What have I done?" Then he slammed the door behind him.

11

ALEX JUST LOST the best damn thing he's ever had in his life.

Nicole methodically grabbed the rungs on the fire escape that belonged to the building across the back alley from the auction house, her destination the roof.

That he'll ever *have*, she added for good measure.

Only her heart wasn't rallying to the cry. The small but important organ felt heavier than her bodyweight squared and she was amazed that she could move at all.

One rung at a time.

Nicole's black Lycra pants allowed her the mobility she needed, while the close-fitting long-sleeved top covered her pale skin and allowed her to blend in with the darkness as she climbed up the side of the building. As with everything else, the key to success was speed. And since she was climbing the fire escape from the opposite well-lit street side, the risk of being seen was high, despite the late hour. Say a neighbor from one of the apartments across the street spotted her. They would look, but if they so much as blinked, she would already be gone, making them question their own eyesight.

As for the residents in the building itself...well, if anyone spotted her from there, she could always play like she was the spurned lover of one of the upper-floor occupants back to get her things and, *shhh,* could they please not say anything?

She hoisted herself up to crouch on the iron-wrought steps then quickly ascended the three flights to the roof as quietly as possible. Only when she leapt over the brick and concrete lip did she allow herself to take a breath.

The only problem was that when she did, images of Alex's accusing face filled her mind.

"I want you to give me the jewelry now, Nicole."

Naturally, she'd thought he'd been referring to the Tiffany pieces. He'd seemed puzzled when she'd said she'd delivered them back to Mrs. Nessbaum's doorstep herself first thing that morning.

But he hadn't been referring to that jewelry. Rather, he'd been talking about a set important to his mother that had come up missing from his family's house yesterday.

Nicole slid to sit on the roof and straightened her supple black suede boots. The louse thought she'd stolen his mother's jewelry.

What kind of luck did she have that something would come up missing while she was present and she'd had nothing to do with it? The odds were astronomical. And seemed to reinforce her earlier fear that there was no way anything permanent could work between her and Alex. Only that fear was no longer a fear. It was a heartaching reality.

And, oh boy, did her heart ever ache in a way that it never had before. It choked off her breath and nearly paralyzed her with the intensity of its slicing pain.

She swallowed hard. Somewhere in the back of her mind a voice told her that Alex's assumption was only to be expected. After all, she was a thief and when something popped up missing, it made sense that she would be the first person looked at.

Still...last night they had experienced so much together. Come together in a way that was so honest, so moving she didn't think she'd ever be the same again.

Then there had been the talk with her father. A conversation that had ignited a hope she couldn't remember ever feeling before. Hope that she and Alex could have more than just today.

A hope that was crushed the moment she looked into his handsome face and saw the mistrust in his eyes, the disenchantment bracketing his full mouth and the unbending stiffness of his posture.

Nicole rested the back of her head against the short wall of the roof then closed her eyes. One of the first rules you learned when you chose a life of crime was to know when you should cut your losses and run. She'd known standing there in Alex's kitchen, staring at him in sadness and shock, that nothing she could have said or done would have changed his mind.

But nothing had prepared her for the staggering loss.

Loss of hope.

Loss of Alex.

She lifted a gloved hand to push her hair back and found her fingers shaking. Not good.

The problem was her exterior was mirroring the condition of her interior, her shattered, shaking emotional state. While she might look all business in her dark cat suit, the truth was she wanted to blend with the darkness and disappear altogether.

A dull clang sounded from the direction of the alley across the roof. She traversed the gravel-covered rooftop in a crouched position, checking to make sure her pistol was still tucked into the back of her waistband, then grabbed the low wall and slowly moved to look over the side.

A truck had pulled into the alley right outside the auction house. Benniman Moving Co. was stenciled on the side. She tried but failed to get a look at the driver. She'd bet dollars to donuts that there was no such moving company. Or if there was, they'd report one of their trucks stolen first thing in the morning. Either way, that meant the people who had driven it into the alley were more than likely the thieves she'd predicted would hit tonight. A band of thieves led by the untouchable Dark Man.

She tugged her gloves on tighter.

Untouchable until tonight...

ALEX SAT in the front seat of the unmarked van staring at the Johnstone's mammoth Greco-Roman-style house until his eyes hurt.

P.I. Kylie Capshaw uncapped a thermos and took a drink straight from the source rather than pouring the contents into the cap cup. She held it out to him. "Want some?"

Alex looked at the pretty blonde. Really looked at her for the first time. He'd been contracting with her company for the past five months, but there had been little excuse for personal contact.

He'd guess Kylie was a couple of years shy of thirty, but her blue-green eyes seemed better suited to someone at least twice her age.

They'd been sitting outside the Johnstone's empty house—he'd known they were in Europe for an extended holiday, thus the reason he'd chosen their house as ground zero—waiting for D.M. to hit for the past three hours straight and aside from some preliminary professional exchanges at the onset, he and Kylie had barely said two words to each other. Of course, Alex was preoccupied with thoughts of another woman, and with every minute that ticked by on his watch, he felt worse and worse.

His sister had taken the jewelry to be cleaned.

He still couldn't believe it.

Shit.

But what upset him more was that Nicole hadn't offered up more than a token fight. She'd merely collected her things and left.

What did that say about her? And what did it say about him and where their relationship might have been heading?

Kylie began to take back the proffered thermos. He reached for it. "Thanks."

He could use some coffee right about now. Something, anything to kick-start his slowly beating heart.

He coughed when he found himself swallowing more than coffee.

Kylie chuckled quietly.

"What's in this?"

She accepted the thermos back and handed him a napkin. "Oh, about one cup of coffee and three cups of Bailey's Irish Cream."

He stared at her as he dried some overflow from his hand. "You always drink on the job?"

She smiled as she screwed the lid back on. "Always."

She neither offered up excuses or explanations, reminding him of Nicole.

Of course, had Kylie been wearing a flowery dress and doing the cha-cha in her seat she probably would have reminded him of Nicole. Seemed he was completely incapable of prying the maddening woman from his mind.

Kylie sighed. "Nothing." She looked at him in the dark. "I have to tell you again, I don't think anyone's even paying attention to this place. Aside from us, of course. The most action I've seen in the past four days is the gardener pruning the annuals bordering the walk there."

Alex had been so distracted he hadn't even thought about the case. All he seemed capable of doing was cursing himself and wondering where Nicole had gone after she'd left his place. And hoping she was all right.

Kylie squinted at him. "Are you okay?"

"Hmm?" Alex looked at her blankly.

She gestured at where he was still wiping his hand. "You don't seem all there."

Oh, he was all here, all right. The problem was he was wishing he were somewhere else and with someone else.

"Fine. I'm fine," he said absently, staring out at the empty estate house again. All the lights were on timers, the security system armed and the only sound to be heard was the chirping of crickets.

"Can I ask you a question?" he said quietly.

Kylie shifted in her seat. "Sure," she said, although she didn't sound all that sure. "Go ahead." She smiled. "After all, nothing says I have to answer it."

He grinned at that. "What is it with you bad girls? I mean, are you raised being wary of everyone?"

"Excuse me?"

He shook his head. "Nothing. That wasn't my question. I, um, was just thinking aloud."

Silence stretched between them as Alex searched for a way to tactfully ask his question. He cleared his throat. "Tell me, what would it take for you to settle down?"

Kylie's eyes widened, then she slowly smiled. "Are you proposing?"

"Sadly, no."

"Good, because I would have turned you down flat."

"Is it something I said?"

She shook her head and reached for a bag of chips on the dash. "Uh-uh. It's just that I've pretty much figured out that the marriage route isn't part of my personal plan."

He waited for her to continue. She didn't. Instead she crunched on potato chips then washed them down with the Bailey's-laced coffee.

"Is there any particular reason for that?" he asked.

She looked down, seeming unnaturally interested in the chip bag. "Let's just say that when a girl gets burned often enough, well..." She shrugged.

"You've been burned a lot?"

"You could say that." She laughed without humor and held out the bag. He shook his head and she put it back on the dash. "Not a lot of men can handle what I do for a living, you know?"

Alex guessed that not many men could handle her, period.

Just like he couldn't handle Nicole.

He sank back in the seat and blew out a long breath. "They don't know what they're missing," he said absently. "The guys who can't handle what you do for a living."

She stared at him. "And your girl...she's probably wishing you'd call her."

He gave Kylie a lopsided smile. "Trust me, I'm the last person she wants to hear from right now."

"Which means you're the first one who should call." She picked up a pair of binoculars from the dash and scanned the quiet neighborhood and the area around the house. She lowered them a little and looked at him.

Alex realized he was staring. "I just think you may be right."

Kylie grinned. "I'm always right."

JUST A LITTLE PEEK...

Nicole duckwalked to the far corner of the roof, paused for a moment, then looked over the side at the truck below. There was someone in the cab, sitting behind the wheel, but given the angle at which the vehicle was parked, there was no direct light to make out more than a shadow.

Damn.

There was a brief flash of light, then a point of red burned bright before dimming again.

A cigarette. He was smoking a cigarette.

She watched as smoke curled from the open window up over the roof of the truck cab, then she sat back.

What was he waiting for?

She pushed back her shirt sleeve. Just after 2:00 a.m. At this time of night she should be in bed...with Alex.

She jammed her eyes shut. Hot, untrusting men and soft, rustling sheets were the last things she should be thinking about right now. The only problem was, every time she breathed, she caught herself pining over Alex.

And pining was about the word for it, too.

She grimaced and tugged her sleeve to cover her watch again.

She was going to have to go down.

She looked over the side again to find the driver pitching his cigarette out the window, producing a wide arc of sparks. Nicole followed the path then nearly hit the gravel when she looked back to find the driver had exited the vehicle and appeared to be looking directly up at her.

Great. Just great. Here she was a seasoned pro and she was making mistakes usually reserved for amateur night.

She hurried back across the rooftop toward the fire escape, not stopping again until she stood on the sidewalk below.

There was no traffic at that time of night. As busy as New York and New Yorkers were, even the city and its occupants had to sleep sometime. And on Monday, it was now. Checking her gun, her cell phone and her can of industrial grade mace, she walked down the block, keeping close to the shadows while she caught her breath. Within three minutes she hugged the brick that flanked the alley entrance then slowly moved her head to take in the back of the truck parked some fifty feet down the alley. It hadn't moved.

One of the lights above the auction house garage door went off. Then another. She squinted to see that the driver was pointing what had to be a peashooter at the protected bulbs until the area around the auction house was as dark as the rest of the alley.

That meant that the streetlights behind her spotlighted her like a target.

Nicole slunk to the inside of the alley, keeping close to the wall, and moved in a few feet away from the light.

The driver put the play gun in the truck cab and took out a more sinister piece that looked like it weighed as much as Nicole did. She swallowed hard, thinking the thing could blow a hole a mile wide in the brick she clung to. Not to mention what it could do to her.

She concentrated on keeping her breathing easy as the driver rounded the truck, looked around, then released the clamp keeping the cargo door closed. The door rolled silently open and out jumped four guys dressed all in black.

Whoa.

Five against one.

Even Nicole knew those odds weren't exactly in her favor.

But she'd come too damn far to back off now. Who knew when Dark Man would show up as a blip on her radar again?

She watched the men form a huddle of sorts then scatter, none of them approaching the door to the auction house.

What were they doing?

She edged a little closer to see better, then felt something poke into her back. She blindly reached back to see what was jutting from the wall. Only what she found wasn't attached to the wall, but rather to a man. A very big man.

And this time it wasn't Alex.

"YOU WANT ME TO WAIT?"

Alex climbed out of the van down the street from the auction house. "No. I'm sure nothing's going on here, either. Why don't you go on home, Kylie," he told her. "I'll call you tomorrow and we'll talk about where we go from here."

"Okay." She nodded. "After pulling double shifts the past few days I could use some downtime."

Alex thanked her then watched as her van turned right at the first corner.

He didn't quite know what he was doing here.

Oh, hell, he knew perfectly well what he was doing here. Somewhere nearby Nicole was in shadow waiting for D.M. to make a move for the paintings.

He absently rubbed the back of his neck and eyed the surrounding businesses. Quiet. Everything quiet.

Despite her urgings to do so, he'd never taken the time to case the joint, learn the ins and outs, hadn't even encouraged Nicole to talk to him about what she'd found out, so he was pretty much feeling his way around in the dark.

More than likely D.M. wouldn't go for the front entrance. Previous jobs showed him going from the back, the side, even the roof, but never the front. That was too obvious.

Was there an alley?

He stepped up to the front of the building. Locked steel mesh protected the sparkling windows and the front door. He lifted a hand to shield his eyes from the streetlamps and squinted into the darkness through the right window. A pair of antique armchairs were positioned on either side of a butt-ugly seascape painting showing an angry sea.

Nothing. Not a movement or a beam of light to indicate there was any life in the place.

Then again, there probably wouldn't be. He'd been to auctions here before and knew the main auction room was located near the back. And, of course, the policy listed the vault as being in the basement.

He stuffed his hands deep into his pants pockets and started around the block to check out the alley, his gaze skimming the buildings across the street. If Nicole was indeed staking out the auction house, could she see him right now? And if she could, would she say anything?

Damn, but he'd made a fine mess out of what had been, as Athena had so eloquently pointed out, the best thing that had ever happened to him. His life had resembled a work-related vacuum, the only happenings unrelated to work involving his parents and sister.

Not that he'd noticed.

At least not until he'd knocked on Nicole's hotel room door in Baltimore and found himself staring into the most beautiful, exotic, provocative eyes he'd ever seen.

Almost immediately he'd felt...alive, somehow. He'd become aware of everything he was lacking, and had seen her as the source to fill it. And, oh, had she. She'd snapped back the blinds covering his eyes and made him squint against the light she exposed him to.

But it had been only a matter of time, he supposed,

that his natural instinct to put his hands up to block the dangerous rays would kick in.

And his jumping at the chance to accuse her of wrongdoing had been just the excuse he'd been waiting for.

The sound of metallic scraping ripped him from his thoughts. He slowed his pace, realizing he was near the alley that led to the auction house's back entrance. The way he'd been going, he would have passed the opening without a glance.

Now he tucked his chin into his chest and covertly glanced down the dark passage as he passed.

Jesus.

Nicole was right. D.M. had targeted the auction house.

"I WOULDN'T DO THAT if I were you," Nicole told the goon who had caught up with her in the alley, tied her hands together, then shoved her inside the back of the truck.

The same goon was now taking great pleasure in patting her down for weapons, his hand openly inching toward her groin area. He slid it the rest of the way home and Nicole brought her knee up, catching him squarely in the nose.

He made a garbled sound then stumbled back a few inches, grabbing his face.

"I warned you," she muttered under her breath, earning laughs from the others in there with them.

She yanked on the plastic tie binding her hands together behind her back, but there was no getting out of it without something sharp to cut it with.

Three other goons were also in the truck, but she didn't know if Dark Man was one of them.

The one she'd kneed regained his equilibrium and straightened to his full height, glaring at her in the dim light from an electric lantern. He made a low sound in his throat that resembled a growl and advanced on her, apparently determined to pay her back. Nicole shoved her back against the side of the truck and braced herself.

An arm caught her would-be assailant across the shoulders. "Leave it. You've got work to do."

Dark Man?

Nicole swallowed hard, thinking it probably was.

The other three goons extinguished the light then opened up the door and climbed out. The one remaining turned the light back up just enough for Nicole to make out his eyes behind the black ski mask.

"So finally we officially meet, Ms. Nicole Bennett."

Her heart hiccupped in her chest. He knew her name. Not good.

"I'd say the pleasure was all mine but, you know, one ski mask looks the same as any other," she said coolly.

A flash of teeth through the mouth hole, then the mask was lifted and she found herself staring directly into the face of Dark Man.

She only wished the experience made her feel better.

QUICK WORK with a padlock cutter and the three men who had climbed from the back of the truck were rushing inside.

Alex looked around from where he was standing in the shadows at the end of the alley, wondering where in the hell Nicole was. No matter how angry she was with him, she'd acknowledge his presence. Wouldn't she?

He shuddered in apprehension.

The police. He needed to call the police.

He felt around his pockets for his cell phone. Damn. He must have left the blasted thing in Kylie's van. A hell of a lot of good it would do him there.

He slipped back out onto the street and looked up and down it. There was a payphone two blocks up and to his left. Short of randomly knocking on people's doors and hoping they would let him use their phone, it was his only option.

A quiet approach. That's what they needed to make. No sirens. No flashing lights. They needed to block off both entrances to the alley and the front simultaneously before making their move or else Dark Man would slip through his fingers yet again.

He silently cursed the length of New York City blocks then finally drew even with the phone and snatched the receiver from its cradle. A vehicle screeched to a halt at the curb and the passenger door swung open.

"Good thing I did a little snooping around before calling it a night. Looks like you could use my help," Kylie called to him. "Get in."

Alex was only too happy to oblige.

THINGS WERE GOING from bad to worse too quickly for Nicole's liking.

Twenty minutes after D.M. had officially introduced himself, three other goons were back and pushing her into the dark confines of the auction house vault. With her hands still tightly bound behind her back, there was little she could do but give an occasional shove that only succeeded in angering the guy in charge of her.

She was only glad that he wasn't the same one she'd smacked in the nose with her knee or else she'd be the one getting the shoves. Likely headfirst into the crates surrounding them.

She tripped over something in the dark.

"Would somebody turn on a light, please?" she said between gritted teeth.

A door closed behind them and a light was switched on. She looked down to see what she'd tripped over and nearly screamed when she saw the guard she'd paid for information the other day. His face stared up at her sightlessly. Stone-cold dead.

Nicole quickly swallowed the bile rising in her throat as she spotted two other bodies in the same condition.

She'd never seen a dead person this close before. It looked like someone had pulled their plug, letting out every bit of air so that their muscles and skin hung slack and gray.

"Oh, God," she murmured.

D.M. chuckled. "What's the matter, Ms. Bennett? Don't like seeing the results of your handiwork?"

She stared at him. He'd put his mask back on, likely in case there were hidden cameras trained on the area that they hadn't identified.

"That's right. You killed these three men. In cold blood."

Nicole's knees felt suddenly weak, but she strengthened them and straightened her shoulders. Why was she getting the impression that this theft was less about the paintings and more about her?

"Excuse me, but did I accidentally run over your dog or something?" she asked. "Because it sounds like you're carrying a grudge and I'm the unlucky recipient of it."

"Let's just say that we share some people in common."

"No, I'd say let's get specific because I've had just about as many vague jabs as I can take for one night."

"Okay, then. As you wish."

Dark Man seemed to appreciate a painting that one of his goons had broken out of its crate and was checking for security bands, anything that might help someone locate the painting in case of theft.

"Do you recall a woman by the name of Christine Bowman, Ms. Bennett?"

Oh, boy, did she.

Christine Bowman's name seemed to be coming up a lot lately. She was the thief who had stolen a small fortune in uncut diamonds from the diamond district right here in New York, leaving two dead security guards in her wake. Nicole had followed Christine to St. Louis and acted like she was the regular housekeeper of the mansion Christine had rented, pleading with her when Christine might have sent her away that Nicole needed the money to take care of her six kids.

Then after dodging and confronting a green but savvy St. Louis P.I. named Ripley Logan, she'd made off with the diamonds, but not before seeing Christine arrested for the original theft and involvement in the murders of the two guards.

D.M. stepped to loom over her, his gaze raking her

face. Nicole could feel the rage emanating from him. "She was my wife. Well, technically she still is, but you can understand how her being behind bars for life would restrict such a relationship."

Nicole wished she could find the stop button so she could get off this scary ride.

"Yes, Nicole, consider this payback time," he said, moving so the mouth of his mask hovered above her ear.

She shuddered, knowing she was in for it good this time.

She looked everywhere but at the man doing a fine job of intimidating her. "Aw, I'm flattered. You mean to tell me you did all this for little ol' me?" She forced herself to stare directly into his eyes when he pulled back to look at her. "You should have just killed me. It would have been simpler."

He grinned, nothing but teeth in a jagged black hole. "Yes, but it would have been much less satisfying."

Nicole swept her leg out, catching him forcefully at the ankles. He went down like a ton of bricks. Hands still bound behind her back, she ran for the door.

12

ALEX HEARD the commotion inside the vault and used it to cover his quick, silent entrance through the thick door. He ducked off to the side behind a couple of high crates just in time to see a masked man grab Nicole's hair and jerk her backward from where she'd apparently been trying to flee.

The masked man put his face next to hers and swore vehemently while Alex instinctively reached for a gun that wasn't there.

Damn it, why hadn't he thought of taking his piece with him when he left the loft? Then he remembered why. He'd been so damn preoccupied by everything that had happened that day, he hadn't been thinking much at all. First Nicole's disappearance from the loft. Then his mother's jewelry being stolen. If that weren't enough, he'd had to sit through his sister telling him the jewelry hadn't been stolen at all, but was out being cleaned, and that he was a moron for ever having believed Nicole could have taken it.

"She's the best damn thing that's ever happened to you," his sister's words echoed in his mind, haunting him again.

Out of sheer stupidity, he'd pushed Nicole out of his life. He eyed the entrance to the vault. But now, with all his power, he would make sure she wouldn't be taken away from him for good.

NICOLE'S EYES watered fiercely as D.M. yanked mercilessly on her hair.

"Try something like that again and I'll make sure torture is included in the repertoire," he whispered into her ear.

She whipped her head away and thought about smacking the back of her head against his nose. The problem was that she'd probably get no farther than she had a moment ago. The other three goons were on alert now, closely watching her even as they readied their bounty.

She was finally released then shoved into a growing pile of discarded crates.

"You know, the authorities are onto you," Nicole said between clenched teeth.

"The authorities will never be able to connect the dots. I'm too good."

Nicole merely grinned, insinuating that she knew something he didn't.

He bit. Big time.

"Where'd you get this information? From your ex-cop boyfriend?"

Nicole's throat narrowed. How did D.M. know she and Alex were...had been involved?

Realization swept over her skin, chilling her straight through to the bone. All along it hadn't been Alex who was watching her. It had been D.M.

Nicole suddenly felt dizzy.

Don't you dare pass out. Don't you dare.

She shifted until she could easily get into a standing position. Strange, it seemed, that just a few hours ago she had thought law enforcement and the state prison system her greatest enemies. As she stared into the covered face of the man who had spent Lord knows how long arranging this setup, it was sobering to think that she hadn't even considered something like this might happen.

She squinted at him.

Why had he taken so long, anyway? Why hadn't he forced her hand before now?

"Which others do you want, boss?" one of the goons asked.

D.M. silently towered over her, appearing not to have heard the question. Then he said, "The crates to the left. All of them."

Nicole's skin crawled under his intense scrutiny.

He finally turned away.

She sagged against the broken crates, relieved.

Broken crates...

Her heartbeat accelerated. If she worked a piece of wood into the plastic restraint and twisted...

She'd cut her hands off at the wrist.

Unless she could find a way to protect her wrists.

She covertly scanned the debris to her left and right, finding several wood pieces thin enough to work between her and the tie. But would the wood hold under the stress?

Well, she wasn't very well going to find out unless she tried, was she?

She scooted over to her right where the most promising pieces lay and began methodically feeling her way through the pile of rubble.

Suddenly, the tie gave.

Nicole gasped.

"Shhh," Alex whispered from somewhere behind the crates.

Oh, God, Alex!

Nicole's stomach pitched to her feet then back again. *Alex had come for her.*

Instantly forgotten were his accusations. The memory of the awful way he had looked at her. Her fear that she had made a very bad mistake getting involved with him. All of it left and was replaced by mind-numbing relief.

"When I say run," Alex murmured, though she had yet to see him. "Run."

She nodded once to indicate she'd heard.

She sat with her hands clasped behind her back rather than tied and tried to restrain the smile that threatened. Who would have thought she'd live to see the day when she was glad Alex was once a cop?

D.M. was supervising the opening of the last of the paintings and she hoped that Alex, who proved he liked to go slow in so many ways, understood the word "fast."

But even as she waited for the go-ahead, she plotted her path out. Dart to the left, duck behind the crates there, then make a mad dash for the vault door.

That was the part that concerned her. The mad dash for the door. Because once she moved, she'd become a target and that stretch was the most open, left her the most vulnerable.

She heard a sound and jumped when all three goons dropped what they were doing and aimed highly sophisticated, mammoth weaponry toward the vault door. Oh, boy. If that was what she was in for, no crate was going to save her.

"Whoa," the newest addition said, holding his

hands up in the air. "No need for the warm welcome. It's just me."

"Run!" Alex shouted from behind Nicole.

She began to do just that when the new arrival pulled back his mask to prove his identity, pinning her to the spot.

Every molecule of air left her body as she stared at her brother. "Jeremy..."

WHAT IN THE HELL WAS SHE DOING?

Alex stood behind the open vault door, ready to smash it into the new arrival and dash out behind Nicole. But he'd issued the command for her to run and now she stood as if a magnetic force held her to the ground staring at the man who had caused the distraction he'd been waiting for.

He squinted at Nicole's shocked expression then turned to look back at the man. It looked like...it was the guy he saw her speak to at the coffee shop last week.

Damn it all to hell. If they were going to get out of here before the police arrived and things really started getting hairy, the time was now.

"Jeremy," Nicole said, still not having moved.

"Jesus...what the hell is going on here?" the man said as he saw Nicole. He stalked over to the man who appeared to be running things. "What's my sister doing here?"

Sister? The man was Nicole's brother?

Alex wondered if there were any more surprises in store for him tonight.

The man in charge calmly laid his hand on Jeremy's arm. "She's here for the same reason you are," he said, pulling a handgun out of the back waist of his black slacks. "You're both going down for this crime." He shrugged. "And, of course, the murder of the three guards."

Alex's heartbeat thundered through his veins. Just when you thought things couldn't get worse.

"What—"

Jeremy didn't get a chance to finish his thought as the masked man brought the heel of his gun down on the other man's head. Jeremy fell to his knees, obviously trying to hold onto consciousness. When it looked like he was regaining his bearings, the masked man hit him again. Jeremy hit the floor, out cold.

"Leave him alone!" Nicole shouted, getting to her feet and revealing that she was no longer bound.

She picked up a plank of wood and appeared to aim for the man's head. He ducked, but it hadn't been his head she was after, rather the hand that held the gun. The heavy metal fell to the cement floor then slid until it smacked up against the wall.

Her target roared then caught her around the waist causing her to drop the wood. She fought him, bringing her heel down on his instep and elbowing him in the solar plexus but nothing succeeded in getting him to relax his grip. Instead, he shifted his right hand until he was gripping her throat.

Not good.

Alex began to rush forward when he heard someone else enter from the vault door. "Let her go, slimebag."

Slimebag?

Alex watched as Kylie stepped in from the same direction Jeremy had entered, holding a mean-looking stun gun that crackled as she pointed it at Nicole's assailant where he stood twenty feet away. Would the wires reach?

That got the other goons' attention and they turned on her with their own very real guns, that shot very real bullets, from any distance.

Alex felt ridiculously like he'd been caught in an Arnold Schwartzenegger movie and he was the only one not holding a gun.

Nicole reached into the back of her own slacks and pulled out her small caliber pistol, then pressed the muzzle against her assailant's temple.

Yup. Definitely the only one.

"Tell your friends to drop their weapons," Nicole ordered.

Nobody moved.

"Now!" she shouted.

"I'd do what the lady says." Alex stepped out of the shadows so that the men were now flanked. Of course he wasn't armed, but he thought the best course of action to take right now would be to appear that it didn't matter. He crossed his arms and grinned at the four thieves. Then he shrugged. "You know, unless all of you want to kiss your asses goodbye."

Silence. Then Alex could have sworn he heard a quiet chuckle. A chuckle that grew louder as each second passed.

He narrowed his eyes on the one holding Nicole.

"Bravo, Cassavetes," the man said, sounding remarkably familiar. "You know, I really didn't think you had it in you." He moved until he was facing Alex. Nicole made a choking sound and fought to keep her pistol pressed against his temple. "You know, there was a running bet around the company that you quit the force because you couldn't hack it."

The company?

Realization dawned on him at the same time the masked man used his free hand to peel back the mask from his face.

John Carlon.

A man he had worked with at the insurance company for the past year. A man who had reportedly just taken a job out in San Francisco with another company and whose last day was the previous Friday.

Dark Man had been right there under his nose all along.

A flurry of activity sounded as police stormed the building from every entrance. "Freeze!"

A chilling expression came over John's face as he continued to hold Alex's gaze. As if in slow motion, he followed the inside of Nicole's arm up with the backs of his fingers, as if lovingly caressing her. Then he fastened his hand over hers where she held her gun and pulled the trigger.

NICOLE SAT in the back of an unmarked van, her throat raw and tight, her hands shaking as she checked the back of her brother's head. He'd come to right after the police had made the arrests.

She shuddered. Well, after they had arrested Carlon's three goons. John Carlon himself... She shuddered again.

"Here, maybe this will help warm you up." The woman Alex had introduced as P.I. Kylie Capshaw held out a thermos.

Neither of them mentioned that Nicole couldn't possibly need warming up on such a balmy summer night. She sniffed the contents first then took a long pull, feeling the Irish Cream inside immediately go to work on her frayed nerves. Her throat wasn't ready for the alcohol though, and she coughed.

Alex stepped up. "Careful. Kylie likes a little coffee with her Bailey's."

Nicole felt a stab of jealousy at the casual almost fond way Alex spoke of Kylie. She kept her gaze on Jeremy as she handed the thermos back.

"I think I'll leave you guys alone," the P.I. said as she capped her thermos and headed around to the front of the van.

Silence stretched between them. Only a hundred feet to her left flashing lights illuminated the otherwise dark alley as countless N.Y.P.D. officers secured the area and went in and out of the auction house. A vehicle pulled up onto the street to her right. She looked to find it was the county coroner's van.

She shuddered again.

"Sir, the paramedics have arrived."

Nicole blinked to find that a uniformed officer was directing the comment to Jeremy.

"Just one last job," her brother had told her when he'd come to and stared up into her face. "That's all this was supposed to be. Just one last job to cover a down payment on a house for Joanna and Justine and me. I wouldn't have done it except..."

Carlon had made the offer too appealing, Nicole now knew. The reason he had taken so long to set her up was because making her alone pay for Christine Bowman's arrest and life imprisonment hadn't been enough. So he'd thrown first her father into the mix, setting him up in order to chase her from the bushes, then added her brother for good measure, planning to frame them both for not only tonight's heist, but for all his other crimes. And they wouldn't have been able to dispute the allegations because, well, it was a little difficult to talk when you were dead.

If anything good had come out of the night, it was that Nicole was convinced Jeremy was out of the business, this time for good.

Her brother looked at her and she looked at Alex.

"Go ahead. I've got things covered here," Alex said.

Her bother looked back at her. She smiled and nodded, indicating Jeremy could trust Alex. She knew he was a man of his word. He'd promised to keep them safe from prosecution and she knew he'd keep that promise, or die trying.

Jeremy reluctantly got up to follow the officer to the paramedic truck up the block.

Nicole crossed her arms over her chest and hugged herself, wondering if she'd ever feel warm again. She would have thought she'd feel relieved—triumphant, even, at finally catching up with the Dark Man. But when Carlon had squeezed her hand around her pistol...

Alex sat next to her, close enough to touch, but keeping his distance.

Nicole swallowed hard. "Thank you."

He looked at her. "For what?"

"For..." She smiled halfheartedly. "Well, I guess 'everything' about covers it, doesn't it?" She tucked her hair behind her ear. "But the thing I'm most thankful for is your stepping up to keep my brother out of this."

He shrugged. "No problem."

She gazed at him. "Isn't it?"

He considered her long and hard. Then he grinned. "Well, maybe it was a little bit of a problem." The grin vanished. "But nothing I can't handle."

She was beginning to see that there were probably few things that Alex Cassavetes couldn't handle. Which felt odd to admit.

Oh, while she'd been attracted to him from the word go, she'd always thought him on the too-tame side, a man stuck in a groove she was determined to push him out of.

Instead, somewhere down the line she'd begun to understand that Alex's groove wasn't a rut but rather a different way of life. He was solid, thoughtful, loyal, as well as sexy as hell, and she couldn't imagine a situation where he wouldn't be there for those he loved.

And she supposed that was the problem with the two of them and why they couldn't take their relationship any further. He didn't love her. Because in order to have love you had to have trust. And they didn't have that.

"So...you work with Kylie a lot?" she asked quietly.

She felt his gaze on her profile as she watched the paramedics attend to her brother.

After the police had closed in, Alex had sorted everything out in a way that left her and Jeremy out of the spotlight. He'd explained that they worked with Kylie. Nicole had been surprised by how readily Alex's former co-workers had bought the lie. They hadn't even looked twice at her and Jeremy and they would walk away from this without a scratch.

Well, aside from the emotional scar she would have

from having involuntarily killed one man and fallen in love with another.

Alex cleared his throat and shifted where he sat next to her. "I owe you an apology."

Nicole slowly turned her head to look at him. He returned her gaze.

"For what?" she whispered.

"For accusing you of doing something you didn't."

Nicole's heart beat a hopeful rhythm in her chest and warmth began to return to her limbs.

He cleared his throat again and glanced toward the chaos surrounding them. "It seems my sister took my mother's jewelry to be cleaned as part of an anniversary gift for my parents."

Hope vanished. "I see."

"Do you? Because I'm not sure that I do."

She gave a weak smile.

"Do you forgive me?"

She nodded. "That, I can do."

His whole body seemed to relax. He reached for her hand. She moved it away.

"I can forgive you, but it's not enough, is it?"

He squinted at her, apparently trying to make sense out of her words.

She smiled, surprised to find tears burning the back of her eyelids. "If you had told me you believed in me without learning what had really happened to your mother's jewelry, maybe..." She looked everywhere but at him. "You know what's funny?" she whispered. "Just this morning I decided that I didn't want to be a thief anymore. I went to visit my father in prison and..." She didn't know why she was saying what she was; she only knew that she had to. "And I decided that you were more important to me than my career. That you were worth rethinking my entire life." She looked down and laughed quietly. "Strange how things work out, isn't it? Here I was thinking that two simple words like 'I quit' would make all the difference in the world, then you accused me of taking your mother's jewelry and I realized there aren't enough words in the dictionary to change things. Not really."

"Nicole, I..."

She lifted her hand to stop him. "Please. Don't. Just let me say what I have to, okay?"

She held her breath, choosing her words carefully.

"I can't trust you," she said finally. She heard him shift next to her and forced herself to directly meet his gaze. "That's right. I said that *I* can't trust *you*." She pulled her knees to her chest and squeezed. "How can I be sure that next week when something comes up missing, you won't accuse me of taking it? How do I know that you won't question my every move, wondering what I'm up to, or if I'm breaking the law?" Her voice caught and she took a deep breath, trying to ease the pain swirling inside her. Then she whispered, "And I can't trust you with my heart because, even though you won't mean to, you'll break it every day we're together."

On top of everything else that had happened that night, the entire day, the effort it took to say the words seemed to forge a crack right down the middle of her chest.

It seemed to take Herculean effort to push herself from the back of the P.I.'s van. She stepped a couple feet away, then turned, pausing to look at Alex one last time.

What a beautiful man. Not just externally, with his wide chest and infectious grin, but internally. Despite what he must have thought about her, how different their belief systems, he'd opened up to her in a way no one else had before.

But he had kept the one thing she wanted most, his heart, safely hidden away.

She tried for a bright smile and ended up with a sad one. "Go find a nice girl, Alex. One your parents will like. One who would never dream of breaking a law. A nice girl that deserves you. Because I don't."

13

TIME WAS SUPPOSED to heal all....

Wasn't it?

What a crock of bull that was.

A month had passed and Alex was no closer to figuring out why Nicole had told him goodbye than he had been thirty days ago. And rather than his need to do so dissipating, it seemed to increase with every tick of the second hand on his watch.

He pushed from his chair and moved to stand in front of the dry-erase board against his wall. Oh, for all intents and purposes he continued to function the same way he had before Nicole came into his life. Monday through Friday he went into work, put in a full day, then returned home to his loft to eat dinner and watch whatever sports programs were on TV that night. Every Sunday he went to his parents' house.

Dark Man had been stopped. The board was now dedicated to three separate thefts. He pulled the board from the wall then tapped it so it turned to the corkboard side. Images of Nicole filled his vision. Nicole walking down the street looking back over her shoulder, her hair curving against her cheek. Nicole sitting at a coffee shop in a blond wig reading the *Wall Street Journal*, wearing a small saucy smile. Nicole standing on the subway, her hand stretched to the bar above her, the look in her eyes faraway and almost sad.

He reached out to touch that picture. The one of her looking...lost somehow. It was the one image that most closely resembled the look she'd worn when she'd told him goodbye. The expression that haunted both his dreams and his waking hours...when he wasn't thinking about the soft moans and whimpers and exclamations she'd made when they'd made love.

"You're pathetic, Cassavetes. A grade-A moron."

He tugged the photo from its tack and slipped it into his pocket, then began taking the rest of the pictures down. It was time—long past time if you wanted the truth. She wasn't coming back. He knew that now. It might have taken him a while to figure it out, but he wasn't completely thick. A month without contact would be enough to convince anyone.

Ten minutes later he finished then stood staring at the stretch of empty corkboard. He stepped across his office where he'd bought a poster of Manhattan but had never hung it and pinned that up instead, then tapped the board so that it faced the wall again.

The pictures he put into the Dark Man file that still sat on the corner of his desk, then put the file itself into the out-box for his secretary to file in the closed cases section.

A knock sounded at the door. "Alex?"

"What is it, Dorothy?"

She held up an eight-by-ten envelope. "This just came to you from the P.I.'s office."

He frowned. He didn't have anything pending with Kylie. He'd concluded his latest piece of business with her last week over a drink at a bar down on Broadway. He accepted the envelope, cringing as he remembered that she'd talked him into a shot of J.D. and a beer chaser. But it had been more than one shot, hadn't it? And he was afraid he'd said far more than he'd intended about Nicole and the fantastic week they'd had together.

"Thanks, Dorothy," he said when he realized she still stood at the door.

"Don't mention it." She turned to leave.

"Wait," he said. "Has anyone ever called you anything but Dorothy?"

She stared at him as if he had a wart the size of the Bronx on his chin.

"You know, like Dot or something?"

She slowly shook her head. "No. Everyone calls me Dorothy. Just Dorothy."

"Oh."

She quietly closed the door after herself and Alex tossed the envelope marked Personal onto his desk. He collapsed into his chair and swiveled it to look out the window. Someone in the building across the street seemed to be doing the same thing, their feet on their desk where it faced the window. Maybe he should move his desk to face the glass, despite the impracticality of it. When the sun hit, he could always pull the blinds.

He rubbed his face with his hands then sighed. He must have been in really bad shape recently if even his mother felt compelled to ask what had happened to that strangely beautiful woman he'd brought home last month, and said it would be nice to see her again.

He cocked a half smile. His mother wanted to see Nicole again. Unbelievable. Almost as unbelievable as her parents' gradual acceptance of Athena's recent revelation to them.

Of course, guilt could be partially to blame for his mother's attitude toward Nicole. Given that she had thought Nicole had taken her dowry jewelry right along with him. Athena had been forced to spill the beans about her anniversary party plans and she never passed up an opportunity to tell him and their mother how judgmental they both were. Like mother, like son, she was fond of saying as of late. His father remained silent on the entire matter, except when they were alone and he would make the odd comment about what great legs Nicole had.

The anniversary party was in two weeks and they had even more reason to celebrate because his father had told Alex the idea of moving to Greece had been put on the back burner. His mother had even suggested it might be a good reason to give "that Nikki girl" a call and invite her to the party. Or if he didn't want to, his mother could do it if he gave her Nicole's phone number.

He wouldn't have given it to her even if he knew how to contact Nicole.

He swiveled to face his desk again. The envelope from Kylie sat smack-dab in the middle of it. Taking his opener from the lap drawer, he carefully slit the end then dumped the neat one-page letter attached to something onto his desk.

"The picture is for your collection," read a hot pink sticky note stuck to the letter. "And the rest because you're too dumb to do it yourself."

Alex turned the cover letter over and found himself staring at an eight-by-ten glossy of Nicole standing outside a small cottage near water. She had her hair pulled back into a French braid and wore a white tank top and capris and stood on the sand. He squinted at the photo. Was she painting? Cat was curled up on top of a blanket at the foot of the easel.

Alex's heart beat loudly in his ears. He knew the photograph had been taken recently or else Kylie would never have sent it. He pressed his fingers against his temples, pondering that Kylie had been the one to snap the majority of the pictures he'd just taken down from the corkboard. But this one...this picture was completely unlike the others. Where was the black leather? The urban posture? The reckless energy? This Nicole...well, looked almost at peace—if not for the sad, faraway look in her eyes as she stared out at the water.

He quickly detached the letter paperclipped to the photo and read it. Only there was no Dear Alex or date or any other identifying marks except for Kylie's business letterhead.

Name of subject: Nicole Bennett, aka Holly Golightly Harvak.

Alex blinked then read the line again.

No way. There was no effin' way her parents had named her after the Audrey Hepburn character in *Breakfast at Tiffany's.* He looked at the picture, then back at the letter again. No wonder she had a Tiffany complex and had a cat she'd named...well, Cat.

He absently scratched his head as he read through the rest of the background information. What date she was born in Brooklyn. Where'd she gone to school. Sketchy data on her brother, his wife and infant daughter. She'd even named which prison her father was doing time in and noted how often Nicole had visited. He noticed with a sinking sensation that she'd gone for the first time since his incarceration the same day he'd accused her of stealing his mother's jewelry.

Damn.

Then she listed the address of the cottage in the picture.

Westhampton—bought three years ago with money kept in trust for her until age twenty-five. Mother's life insurance policy. Her brother had used his half to open up his own plumbing company.

Alex sat for a long time staring at the documents in his hands. So much he hadn't known about her. So much she'd kept from him. So much he suspected she kept from everyone.

And he cursed Kylie for forcing his eyes open to see it.

HOLLY PARKED her old convertible Volkswagen Bug in her narrow gravel driveway and reached back to gather the bags of groceries she'd picked up. She glanced out at the white, three-room cottage thinking it looked small and lonely and isolated sitting near the edge of the beach all by itself. She glanced at the larger house a couple hundred yards to her left. The cottage had once been a guest house of the owners, but then they'd expanded the house and had no more need for separate guest quarters and had put the cottage on the market three years ago. Nicole had immediately snatched it up, spending almost every penny of the money she'd inherited from her mother to buy the lovely cottage.

She unlocked then shouldered open the door. Cat immediately began twisting around her ankles where he'd been waiting just inside.

"Such a good, good boy," she said, bending down to scratch his ears before walking across the living area that opened into a kitchen/dining room. Everything was done in whites and off-whites. White walls, white ceiling fan, white furniture with white overstuffed pillows. She put the bags down on the butcher-block island and took out a small plant she had bought. She put it in the middle of the dining room table, stood back and looked at the splash of color in the otherwise pristine cottage, then moved it to the coffee table between the sofa and two chairs. She crossed her arms. There. It looked better there.

Given her erratic travel schedule, she hadn't dared buy a plant before now. But since she didn't plan on traveling anytime in the near future, a plant had seemed just the thing to buy.

Cat nipped at her ankle then meowed.

Holly looked at him. "Impatient tonight, aren't you, buddy? Hold onto your knickers, I'll get your food in a minute."

She put the rest of the groceries away, which didn't take much time considering she and Cat were the only ones she was buying for. She stared at a package of pasta in her hands, remembered the last time she'd planned to make pasta, then quickly put the package away in the cupboard.

She would not think about Alex. She refused to.

She jerked open a can of cat food, nudging Cat away from where he tried to put his face directly into the tin.

Until Alex, she'd bought the cheap stuff for Cat. The four-for-a-dollar variety pack that was easy on the pocketbook and that the stray that had come with the house didn't seem to mind. Then Alex had brought the expensive stuff home and Cat refused to eat anything else.

Home...

She paused as she used a fork to put half the can's contents onto a plate. For some reason she had a hard time convincing herself that Alex's loft had never been home. The cave had merely been his apartment. There was no way she could have seen it as a home given the brief time she'd spent there. Yet whenever she thought of him or his loft, the word home always came to mind. More often than her cottage did.

She pushed the plate toward Cat then turned to lean against the counter and take in the cottage.

Maybe it would feel more like home if someone other than her neighbors actually knew she lived there. She grimaced, thinking it a little late for a housewarming party. She absently curved a hand around the side of her neck. Of course, she hadn't given her brother or father the address.

This was her safe haven. Where she'd escaped to whenever she'd needed to reconnect with herself. When the world got to be too much, her line of work too dark, this was where she could just be herself without worrying what others might think. The funny thing was that right after she'd moved in, she'd found herself turning into an opposite version of the Holly she was in the city.

But no matter the clothes she wore, or the color of her couch, she was still essentially the same woman. The person Alex could never love. Not fully. Not unconditionally.

She caught herself rubbing the area over her chest that still hurt so much whenever she thought of the broad-shouldered Greek-American and forced her hand back to her side.

Would there ever come a time when thinking of him wouldn't make her ache to hold him? Long to straddle his hips and welcome him into her body? Want to drive into town and go at him across his desk where the occupants in the building across the street could watch?

Cat finished his meal and rammed his head into her shoulder by way of thank you. She smiled at his loud purr.

"You're welcome, baby."

He leapt down off the counter and she washed his dish and put it in the drainer.

Music. She needed music. Music and a nice, long bubble bath.

Picking up the remote that activated her stereo, she pressed play and her Alanis Morrisette CD switched on. She put the remote back down then headed for her bedroom. In the doorway, she stopped dead in her tracks.

While Alanis sung about a guy who had entered her life uninvited she stared at a small robin's-egg-blue box tied with a white satin ribbon sitting in the middle of her all-white bed.

Someone had been in her house.

The knowledge should have caused some alarm. Should have, but didn't. Because there was only one person who would do this. Only one man who had breezed into her life and turned it upside down and apparently wasn't done with the job.

She slowly approached the bed and sat down on the edge, staring at the box for a long time without moving. She saw Tiffany & Co. written across the top and her heart hiccupped. Slowly, her fingers trembling, she reached out and tugged on the white ribbon. It easily sprung loose and she gently removed the top. A bright, multicolored gem-laden brooch she recognized from the Paloma Picasso collection sat nestled inside.

A soft choking sound escaped from her throat as she stared at the vivid, vibrant piece. She picked up the box and held it in her lap, admiring the way the jewels caught the setting sun and reflected it around the room.

"Read the card."

The softly spoken words came from behind her, from the direction of the bathroom. She didn't have to look to know it was Alex. She heard his voice in her dreams every night.

She looked under the brooch inside the box, then glanced to the bed where a small scrap of paper had been sitting underneath the box.

"You can't hide from me anymore," she read at the same time Alex said the words.

Holly couldn't speak. Couldn't move. She was so overwhelmed by emotion that she could do little more than concentrate on breathing in and out.

"You don't like it," Alex said quietly, not having moved.

Holly slowly blinked. "What?"

"The brooch. You don't like it." From the corner of her eyes she saw him run his hand through his hair in the telltale sign of agitation. "I don't know what I was thinking, buying you jewelry. I mean—"

"I love it," she whispered, interrupting him.

And she did.

In that one moment, she understood why her mother had been so enamored with the simple broach her father had bought her. Why she only took it out on special occasions and got that dreamy-eyed look on her face. She realized what she had been looking for all these years, lifting other people's Tiffany jewelry, trying to find for herself that feeling she'd seen shine from her mother's eyes.

But none of it made sense until now, until this very moment, as she sat with the Tiffany box in her shaking hands, knowing that Alex had not only bought it for her, but that he had bought it out of love.

She tried to blink back her tears, but it wasn't going to work.

She felt Alex's weight on the bed next to her before she realized he had moved to her side.

"Come here," he murmured.

And Holly went.

She burrowed into the wide, comforting arms of the man she loved so much she hurt with it. Let him hold her to that broad chest that had first captured her attention. Allowed him to murmur soft words into her ear.

But most important she finally freed herself to love him. Without fear or reservations. Without wondering what would come tomorrow or the day after or a year from now.

"Marry me, Nicole...Holly. Marry me now. Today. Tonight." He kissed her neck just under her ear. "Marry me so I don't have to wake up without you sleeping next to me. Marry me so I won't go back to the stale, colorless life I led before. Marry me so I can show you how much I love you every day for the rest of our lives."

He brushed his hands down over her arms left bare by her white tank top. She shivered, her nipples instantly growing hard, the apex of her thighs growing hot and wet. She caught her bottom lip between her teeth and nodded.

Alex gripped her chin in his strong fingers. "Was that a yes?"

"Yes," she whispered, laughter bubbling up from her chest. "That was definitely a yes."

_____Epilogue_____

Three months later...

THERE WAS SOMETHING about these hoity-toity parties
that made Alex itch. He liked to think it was because of
the tremendous waste of resources spent on one
night's event. Or even because of the stiffness of the
rented tuxedo he wore. But he knew it was more likely
because it reminded him of the first time he'd surprised Holly in a guest room just like the one he now
stood in.

Or it could be because he'd followed his wife here.
His wife.

Would he ever get used to calling Holly that? It had
taken him long enough to stop calling her Nicole.

Oh, she was definitely not a wife in all the traditional
ways one thought of as a wife. There were no children
on the horizon. Holly refused to even discuss the topic,
she said, until they'd been together for at least five
years. Dinner more often than not was a couple of fried
eggs and bacon, while breakfast consisted of coffee and
maybe a Danish or bagel if either of them felt like running out to get one.

Ah, but the sex...

He heard his buddies make cracks about sex disappearing almost as soon as the "I do's" were exchanged.
Not in his case. Definitely not in his case. The drugstore

down the street was having a hard time keeping up with their demand for rubbers. And he was already considering investing in a stronger bed.

He cracked open the door a little farther and looked out on the Polansky's upstairs hallway. The door to the master bedroom was still closed. A good sign. He glanced at his watch. Then again, maybe not. He didn't feel like waiting around all night to see if his wife planned to make off with Mrs. Polansky's Tiffany jewelry.

He silently cursed. Holly probably wouldn't be very happy to see him here. Hell, he wasn't sure being there was a good idea, either. But for the past three months she'd seemed content to hang around decorating his loft following their simple wedding in his parents' backyard on his parents' thirty-fifth wedding anniversary. He'd been half afraid she'd change all the black to white like her cottage. Instead she'd shocked the hell out of him by inviting his mother and Athena to help her and the place looked...well, it looked more like a home than it ever had before.

Then, tonight, Holly had gotten up after a dinner of boxed macaroni and cheese, kissed him on the cheek and told him she'd see him later. After sitting for five full minutes in shock, he'd secretly followed her. First to a bus station where she'd taken a bag out of a locker. Then to the ladies' room where she'd gone in looking like Holly and come out looking like the blonde he'd surprised in Baltimore. In fact, he thought it was the exact same getup. Then he'd followed her on a train all the way out to Westchester to the house he was in now.

Movement in the hall. He leaned closer to the door and watched as a woman decked out in purple velvet looked around then picked the lock on the master bedroom and ducked inside.

"Roddy, why don't you tell our contestant here what he's won?"

Alex grinned at the sound of Holly's voice behind him.

She slid her arms around him and her hands immediately dove south. He caught her marauding fingers in his.

"What are you doing here?" he asked.

She caught his earlobe between her teeth then released it. "I think that should be my question." She stroked him through his trousers despite his restraining grip. "What's the matter, dear husband of mine? Don't trust me?"

The words caused a moment of panic to shoot up his spine. Her belief that he could never trust her had been what had chased her away once. He unconsciously tightened his grip on her wrists. He never, ever wanted that to happen again.

"I missed you," he whispered.

She laughed again. "Don't worry, baby. I'm not here to steal anyone's jewels," she said, grabbing his. "I'm here to stop them from being stolen."

Alex swallowed thickly, his erection throbbing almost painfully. "Come again?"

"You heard me right. My brother Jeremy's working part-time for an old friend of ours, Bruno Demasi. He operates a security firm." She shrugged, jiggling her breasts against his back. "The baby's sick so I'm filling in for Jeremy for the night to keep an eye out at tonight's little soirée." She made a soft sound. "I didn't tell you because I knew you'd follow me. Hmm...who knows? Maybe this job will lead into something full-time."

Alex groaned then switched positions so that he had her pinned face-first against the wall. She made a soft sound of approval and ground her bottom against his arousal even as he hiked her dress up to find, once again, she wasn't wearing any panties.

He hungrily kissed the back of her neck. "Tell me, how is it that I want you more and more each time I see you?"

She caught his fingers where they rested against her soft, freshly shaven mound then guided them through her slick flesh. "Mmm...maybe because you love this?"

He caught her chin in his free hand and turned her head so he could kiss her. "No. I think it's because I love you."

Unlike the first time they'd done this in Baltimore, Alex had no plans to pull back. They were married. Husband and wife. Certainly they were entitled to...certain privileges.

He unzipped his fly and sheathed himself with a condom she provided.

"I'm afraid you're not doing your job very well," he whispered into her ear then absorbed her shiver. "Someone is stealing the host's jewels even as we, um, speak."

"No, she's not." She smiled, dipped her fingers into her cleavage, then pulled out a diamond necklace. "Because I already have them."

Alex thrust into her to the hilt, wondering how a bad girl could be so very, very good. And thanked the powers that be that she had ever agreed to do anything as conventional as become his wife....

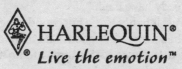

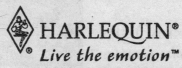

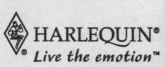